MW01135297

CRUISE

SAVAGE DISCIPLES MC #6

DREW ELYSE

Go for a cruise
with the president!

This one is dedicated to you.
All of you amazing people
that have stuck with the Disciples
even when they act like a bunch of assholes.
Thank you.

It's been one hell of a ride.

PROLOGUE

Stone

I SHOVELED in a forkful of eggs thinking I was becoming a masochist.

It was high past time for me to stop dragging my ass to that diner four days a week. Christ, after that first time stopping in to grab a bite, I should have gotten on my bike and not come back.

Instead, I developed some sick fucking need to torture myself incessantly.

Across the dated countertop I sat at—the same damn place my ass was parked every time I came in—she was singing. She did that a lot. It was always quiet, just barely audible from my spot, and eaten up by the room before it could get to any of the tables.

Today, it was "Delta Dawn."

I knew the song, though I wondered how the fuck she did. It had to be about as old as me. My mom listened to it when I was growing up, but it wasn't a new one even then. Forty-odd years later, it was surprising a girl in her twenties would know it, let alone be singing it quietly while she worked.

In her twenties, I repeated the thought to myself the way I did every time I had it.

Even as I did, I couldn't tear my eyes off of her. Not that that was anything unusual. How the hell she hadn't cottoned on, I didn't know. Then again, Genevieve was a woman the likes of which were rare these days.

Evie had told me a lot in the months I'd been planting my ass on the stool in front of her four times. The only reason I skipped three days every week was because she didn't work them. The food she set down in front of me each time was fine, but it wasn't what kept me coming back. It was her. She was sweet as sugar and for some reason seemed to take to me. This meant I got a lot of her sweet directed my way when I took up residence at that counter. She'd talk about what she had going on, how she was studying to be a nurse, her roommate, crazy shit that happened there at the diner. She'd talk about whatever came to her, and I'd soak up every damn word.

What she hadn't said—and I hadn't asked because I was smart enough to know that it was dangerous ground for my own self-control—was how the fuck she came to be the woman she was. That being, a woman who was cute, gracious, caring, funny, but more importantly, sheltered.

I knew it the first time she'd taken the gamble on talking to me, and she'd asked about my cut. It wasn't like I never got questions about the Savage Disciples MC patch on my back. Hell, it wasn't even like I didn't get those from a whole lot of folks who knew nothing about the life. It was the blatant curiosity that shone in her eyes—a look I'd seen more than a few times since—that verged on wonder. Like a bunch of bikers were the stuff of fairy tales or some shit.

"Top you off, Mr. President?" the object of my obsession asked on a light, ringing laugh.

Yeah, she'd started calling me "Mr. President" when I'd explained that part of the cut to her.

Christ, she was dangerous.

I gave her a lift of my chin, which got me a smile I forced myself not to fully take in as she topped off more coffee into my mug.

"Thanks, babe."

The words earned me another smile, this one softer.

That right there might be the biggest indicator she was sheltered.

She'd told me once, amid her talking about the nursing program she was doing, and how she wished she'd been able to start right out of high school and already be working in the job she'd wanted since she was young, that she'd just recently turned twenty-five. I wouldn't deny that there were twenty-five-year-olds out there that'd smile at me and do a fuck of a lot more. I wasn't in my twenties— or my thirties—anymore, but I could still get a lot of women of a lot of different ages in my bed. Patch chasers or party girls, that "President" stitched onto the front of my cut could get me a taste of a variety of flavors.

Evie wasn't one of those.

A girl like Evie, with the air of innocence that hung

around her, had no business smiling at the gruff, former marine, old-enough-to-be-her-father president of the local motorcycle club.

And that asshole had no business coming around, drinking in all the sweet that was her, and dreaming about what it would be like to get a taste.

"Time to make the rounds," she announced, moving her lithe body around the counter to go check on the two occupied tables in the joint.

I had to curl my hand into a fist so tight my knuckles protested to keep from turning where I sat to watch her move. It was a battle I fought every time I was there. If I had to put a number on it, I'd say I was at about a forty percent success rate. The other sixty percent of the time, I'd end up engraining her courteous smiles, the flair of her waist, the way her hips moved with her steps into my head. Like I didn't already have a million images of her stored away up there, making certain the torture I came here and subjected myself to didn't stop when I walked out the door.

By the time Evie finished her rounds, including delivering bills to both tables, I was finished eating. I'd even gotten out the cash to cover my meal—since I ate there so often I already knew what the damage would be. I told myself again and again that I should get my ass up and just call out a goodbye as I left.

Sticking with the theme, I didn't listen to my own good advice.

Which was why I was still sitting at that damn bar

when she was back behind it, standing right across from me with a smile on her face that had turned tight. I didn't get it, not as I watched her grab the rag she used to wipe down the tables, not as she set about cleaning the unmarred stretch of counter in front of her.

"So...um...any plans this weekend?" There was a faint, nervous tremor to the words.

"Nothing much," I answered, keeping my voice level.

Her anxiety set me on edge. It wasn't like her. She wiped the same spot repeatedly as she turned over whatever she was about to say.

"I was wondering—you know, if you're not busy and all—if you'd want to...I don't know...get dinner," she stumbled out. "Or something."

Fuck.

Fuck me.

Here I'd been thinking all this time that I needed to let go of this attachment. Never, not even once in the craziest shit my brain thought up when I didn't check myself, did I think that the tables would turn.

She had no business, not a fucking lick, asking me out.

And now it fell on me to correct that problem, even when I wanted nothing more than to take her up on her offer.

Fuck.

The time had come. No more avoiding this shit. No more convincing myself it was fine.

This was the end.

"Kills me to do this, you gotta know that, but I'm gonna have to say no."

It sounded like a line, a bullshit way to ease the rejection. I wanted to rip the words back, choke on them if I had to when I watched her face fall as they sank in. She thought I wasn't interested. She honestly fucking thought I'd been coming in all this time for…what? The food? The atmosphere?

No, I'd been there day after day because she was the most magnificent thing I'd ever laid my eyes on and that didn't even scratch the surface of all there was to her.

Turning down her sweet invitation burned through me in a way I knew the singed wasteland left behind would never be the same. But I couldn't give her that. She'd push if I did, and I was too fucking weak to keep resisting.

"Oh," she finally breathed in response. "That…that's okay."

It wasn't. Not for her, with the disappointment she tried —and failed—to mask still showing in her eyes. Not for me, with the way it was actually physically painful to hold in all the words I wanted to give her to ease that damage I'd done.

It wasn't okay in the fucking slightest, but it was the right thing to do.

"I'm not the man you should be offering that to," I found myself saying. I should have just kept my mouth shut, taken the blow that was seeing her dejection, and gotten the fuck out. "Shit's me to say it, but it's the truth."

The downturn of her lips, something I'd never seen before that moment, told me she didn't believe a word of it even as she said, "Okay."

As I sat there, watching her avoid looking at me, watching her chin tip down to her slender neck like she was trying to hide beneath her honey-colored hair, I fought the urge to say more. I wanted to talk until I was blue in the face if needed to make her understand, but doing so would be admitting too much.

Instead, I finally forced myself to do what I should have done months ago. I stood, slid the money closer to her for the bill, and I lied.

"I'll see you soon, Evie."

They were the same words I gave her every time I walked out the door, but it was the first time I said them with no intention of making them true.

FOUR MONTHS LATER, as the bars to the cell I'd be calling home for the next year and a half closed for the first time, that lie was the only thing in my head.

CHAPTER 1

Stone

EIGHTEEN MONTHS.

Eighteen months of my life locked up, and now I was free.

Why didn't that feel better?

I took my last walk escorted by the guards, going through all their administrative bullshit. Answering questions, signing shit, getting my possessions-- just the clothes I'd worn the day I surrendered myself to the state--back.

All I could think about was getting the fuck out of there. I wanted to get home, get my bike, and ride until I didn't remember what it felt like only being able to enjoy the fresh air with armed men watching. I needed the wind, the taste of dust in the air, and the roar of an engine instead of hundreds of assholes making a shit-ton of noise at all hours. I knew the brothers were going to want to make a thing of my release, but I wasn't in the mood for some party they'd no doubt throw together for me.

The second I stepped out the gate, I froze. There it

was--freedom. Finally. Dropping my head back, I took a deep breath in.

Then, "Prez!"

Daz. The loud motherfucker.

He was a couple yards away, straightening from leaning against his truck. He had a big, shit-eating grin plastered on his face, and I could already see the black leather dangling from his hand.

My cut. The Disciples patch and the declaration of my position as voted by my brothers.

Mr. President.

Fuck, would she ever get out of my head?

I walked to my brother. I should have known he'd be the one to get me. He also came to see me more than anyone else. I knew it was guilt driving him, something I'd tried to put an end to but hadn't yet managed to do. Now that I was out, I'd have to see to that.

At the same time, I saw to everything else, like the club I'd had to leave behind all this time.

Why, for the love of God, was that cell I'd finally escaped seeming not so bad at that thought?

Daz's arms came up, one reaching for my outstretched hand, one—holding my cut—reaching around to slap me on the back.

"Fucking finally," he muttered as he pulled back, tossing my cut at me.

For the first time since I'd gotten my prospect patch, the worn leather felt foreign in my hand. I put those colors on every goddamned day until I went away. I shrugged it over my shoulders, noticing the difference in the movement as I did. There wasn't a lot to do inside, so I'd bulked up a bit, exercising both to make it clear what I was capable of and to pass the hours.

If even that cut that defined me for years felt wrong, what the fuck was going to feel right anymore?

"It gets easier."

I looked at Daz, who had none of the usual levity the brother was known for in his expression. He'd spent years in lock up, would be spending more now if I hadn't stepped in. He knew from experience where my head was at, even if he hadn't shown a bit of that when he'd been released.

No, the brother had been all about pussy and booze, which we provided him plenty of.

"Everything feels off for a while. A couple months, maybe less since you weren't in as long. You'll get used to it."

It didn't escape me that he said "get used to it" not "get back to normal."

Not wanting to dwell on this shit that was going to be in my head either way, I shot back, "That woman of yours is making a real impact, huh?"

He got my gist. "Fuck you. Asshole," he threw back even as he smiled. Letting the heavy shit drop, he walked to his truck, leaving me to follow.

Without looking back at the building behind me, I did.

"FAIR WARNING," Daz said from the driver's seat as we pulled into town. Hoffman, Oregon looked the same. The place damn near always did. At least that was a comfort. "The old ladies have been gearing up for today for months it seems. Avery's probably cooked up more shit for this than she's stocked the bakery with."

Avery was Daz's woman. She used to be a dancer and manager at the strip club we owned. One of the few ventures the Disciples had a hand in to keep the brothers living comfortably. Now, she'd lived out her dream and opened a bakery. No fucking lie, that shit was a public service. The woman had been sending me baked goods weekly—yes, every single week for the year and a half I was in there, and extras when there were holidays and shit —and I still hadn't tired of it.

"Not feeling much like a party," I told him.

"I get that. Wasn't how I was feelin' when I got out, but I get how you would. They need this though. Those women, the brothers, Avery fucking especially. She's felt responsible every goddamn day for that shit. Doesn't matter what I say. Doesn't matter that it was my fucking fault…"

Daz's knuckles were stark white as he gripped the steering wheel.

Fuck, I needed to get a handle on that shit.

"Two years ago, you made a decision to protect your woman," I cut in. "When they arrested you for that, I made my decision. You'd have been looking at a decade or more with your record versus me sacrificing a few months of my life to keep that from happening. I made my choice, and I don't regret it. Somehow if I ended up back in time, I'd do it all over again. You were needed at home. I had the power to make it happen. You gotta let this go, brother."

"You spent eighteen months in a cell for something you didn't even fucking do," Daz spat.

"And I'd serve eighteen more! I'd let them lock me up in there to rot for the club, or any of you."

The silence in the cab felt like a physical weight pressing in on us.

"We're not your responsibility," Daz said lowly after a few minutes. We were getting close to the clubhouse, and I wasn't sure if I wanted more time to set him straight or to get the fuck out of there as soon as possible.

"I'd have made the sacrifice from the time I got the word 'prospect' on my back. The minute you all voted me the pres, you and the rest of the club became my responsibility."

"That's bullshit."

He could think that. The whole lot of them could, but it wouldn't change anything.

He turned and pulled into the gravel drive outside the clubhouse.

"That's the way it is."

DAZ HADN'T UNDERSOLD IT. The whole club was on hand the second we walked through the front door to the clubhouse. The converted warehouse only amplified the sound of their cheers as I entered.

I took in all of them. My brothers, their women, the handful of kids that had come along over the last few years. It should have felt incredible. It should have been the greatest fucking thing to happen to me in years to see them all. Instead, I saw them all in front of me and I felt more acutely than ever the time that had passed.

Then, I heard a near-screeched, "Uncle Stone!" just before a streak of blond curls and pink came flying at me. I dropped down just fast enough to catch Emmy, Sketch and Ash's daughter, in my arms. She wrapped herself around me tightly, and the tightness in my chest increased at how much she'd grown. She was seven now, her birthday having just passed. It was the second one I'd missed out on.

"You're home," she said, her voice muffled into my shoulder, her grip on me not wavering.

Fuck, I felt those words right in the gut.

"Yeah, little one. I'm home."

CHAPTER 2

Evie

FOR THE FIRST time in twenty-seven years of life, I really was beginning to question if God hated me.

This didn't happen when I'd finally broken down and left home.

It didn't happen my second semester of nursing school when I got a horrific bout of stomach flu the week of finals.

It didn't even happen a couple hours earlier when I'd gone back to my apartment after a long shift to find the locks being changed.

No, it happened after eleven o'clock at night when the alarming amount of smoke my car was making had become too much to ignore, so I'd pulled off onto the shoulder. It happened when I'd stopped, turned off the car, and tried to start it up again and got...nothing.

All I needed now was for the abnormally chilly May night to be capped off with rain to put the demoralizing cherry on top of a nightmare of a day. As someone that generally tried to keep my mind on the bright side, that kind of woe-is-me dramatics said a lot about my mental state.

See, that afternoon, I learned that basically the only person in my life that I thought I could trust had royally screwed me over.

Four years ago, when I left home with two suitcases to my name, and knowing that I wouldn't be welcomed back, I understood I had to be smart. I found a way to pay for school on my own. I found a way to support myself, even if it meant eight hour shifts after a full schedule of classes and practicums.

What I couldn't do was build a backlog of credit in the blink of an eye, and thus I'd made my fatal error: I put my trust in my classmate-turned-roommate, Steph.

Apparently, over the last couple months, she'd decided not to live up to that expectation, something that was made all too evident when I got home that evening.

ALL I COULD THINK as I climbed the three flights of stairs up to my apartment was how badly I wanted to go to sleep. Maybe when I got up there, I'd just call it a night at six-thirty and be done with it.

I shouldn't. I had a final next week that I should be proactive and start studying for. But sleep. Sleep sounded so much better.

Turning to head up another flight, I took a deep breath in with a silent pep-talk not to give into the exhaustion and sit down right there in the middle of the stairwell. When I did, I caught that ever-unpleasant odor of grease that always clung to me after work. At the smell, I decided firmly that a shower would have to come first. I could spend the time in there debating the merits of crawling right into bed afterward.

All thoughts of showers, of sleep, of anything outside of that apartment building vanished when I turned down the hall and saw the building maintenance guy kneeling in front of our door, apparently changing the lock.

Already feeling a sense of dread, I moved toward him. What if something bad happened? What if someone broke in? What about Steph? Was she okay?

"Um, excuse me," I called as I got close.

The man, who I'd seen around the building a few times but never met, turned his attention to me. "Yeah?"

"I was…well…wondering what you're doing?"

He gave me a look like I had to be stupid before he muttered, "Changing the lock."

"Right. I got that. I was more wondering why."

He eyed me, but responded, "Eviction. Not an issue. No one else is being affected."

Eviction?

I couldn't even process what he was saying. I just stood there, staring at him. Eventually, he shook his head and went back to his task. When he did, I mutely turned my eyes to the numbered plaque beside the door, hoping beyond hope that I'd somehow mistakenly ended up outside the wrong apartment despite making the same trek to and from it for two years.

314.

Nope. That was the right one.

But eviction?

We couldn't be getting evicted.

"Um…doesn't there have to be some notice?"

The guy huffed out a sigh as he stopped what he was doing and looked at me with frank impatience. "There was. A few of them. Reminders about the unpaid rent. A warning what would happen if that didn't get paid. Then the actual eviction notice went up on the door. Put it there myself. Now, if you don't mind…"

"But I live here," I blurted.

Steph had told me not to tell anyone associated with the building I was living there since I wasn't on the lease. She said it would just make things complicated. So I hadn't. Right then, I was pretty sure things were already complicated whether I kept my mouth shut or not.

The maintenance guy turned more fully my way, then stated, "Super said there was only one person on the lease. A Stephanie Mixon. Met her once or twice, and she wasn't you."

No, I definitely wasn't Steph. She was six inches taller than me, model thin, and she had black hair and an olive tint to her skin that only made me look paler by comparison.

"Yes, but I live here, too. I pay part of the rent. I don't know if that's against the building policy or anything…"

"Not that I know of, but I'm not in charge of that, either. Do know it's grounds for eviction if someone goes five months without paying rent."

Five months?

Five. Months.

I'd been giving Steph my half of the rent just like always. Heck, I'd gave her extra the last two months because she said things were *tight for her at the moment, that she'd make it up to me by paying more as soon as she could.*

How could things be tight for her if she was just pocketing all the rent money I'd been giving her?

And yet, even as I had the thought, part of me knew. The same part of me that had hesitated when she'd asked me to cover that extra part of the rent. It was the part of me that noticed the way she'd been changing lately, starting about the time that her latest boyfriend came around. He'd made me uncomfortable right from the start. Then, I'd seen him in the living room from the hall while he shot up. He didn't notice me, but I'd given him a wide berth after that, which meant I'd done the same to Steph.

Which apparently gave her the opening to screw me over.

"*I…I don't…*" I stuttered out, then swallowed to give myself a chance to get it together. "*All my stuff is in there.*"

I noticed through my shock and panic that the man in front of me actually started to look sympathetic in the face of my idiocy that he was clearly catching onto.

"*The super's down in his office,*" he offered, his voice noticeably gentler. I didn't even let myself dwell on the shame that might drum up. "*Go down, explain how she screwed you. I can't say what he'll do. There was a thirty-day evacuation notice, which I'm guessing she made sure you didn't see. But maybe he'll let you get in there to get your stuff.*"

Oh, she definitely made sure I didn't see that, but there was so much more I hadn't let myself see. Maybe if I did, I wouldn't be in that position.

"*Right. I…um…thank you,*" I stammered.

NOW, I found myself with all my possessions packed up once again—though I'd added two boxes to the two suitcases—and in the back of a car that was taking me a whole lot of nowhere.

Since it had taken nearly the entirety of my bank account to convince the none-too-pleased building manager to let me into the apartment to get my stuff, I wasn't exactly sure how I was going to get the funds together to get my car moving again, let alone put down a deposit on a new place.

I sighed, the action aching against the tightness in my lungs.

I wasn't going to cry. I wasn't. Tears weren't going to do a thing for me.

Right now, just like every day since I packed my bags and left home, I had only myself to rely on.

I just needed to come up with a plan.

Somehow.

My musings on this were cut off by a throaty sound of an engine. It was loud, much louder than normal cars. It had to be one of those souped-up ones.

A glance in my rearview mirror showed me a single light approaching rather than two.

Then, it slowed and pulled off the road onto the shoulder behind me.

Seeing that, I actually dropped my forehead to my

hands and prayed that this nightmare wasn't about to get worse.

This went on a little longer than I expected, which gave the man time to dismount and walk up to my door. I only looked up and focused back on the situation at hand when he tapped on the window.

My head popped up, and my mouth dropped open.

The dusting of gray contrasting his dark hair at his temples and parts of his less groomed beard was a bit more prominent than it had been. The muscles in his shoulders and upper arms that I could see stood out even more so. But what really stood out was the edge of a hardness to his face I didn't recognize. Still, he was probably the most handsome man I'd ever seen.

Just like he had been the last time I saw him, right after he'd turned me down when I asked him out.

"Stone."

CHAPTER 3
Stone

IT WAS GETTING LATE, but I didn't care.

The only thing that mattered was being back on my Harley. The sound of the wind and the growling engine wasn't enough to drown out my thoughts, but fuck if it didn't at least muffle them.

I'd finally gotten out of the clubhouse after half the crew had to get their kids to bed. Some of the brothers wanted to keep me around, but them I could talk around. They understood the call. It was the one thing any of the Disciples would get. I hadn't been on the open road in too long.

As I drove, I thought about them. All of them. All of the shit I'd missed.

Sketch and Ash's second daughter, Evangeline, was just a newborn when I'd gone down, and now she was starting to talk.

Fuck, Jager and his woman, Ember—another brother, Roadrunner's daughter—had a kid at all. Not that I hadn't known. The two had come to visit to tell me themselves.

But their daughter, Jamie, had been born just over a month ago. I hadn't been there for that.

I knew it did no good to dwell on it all. Tomorrow, I had to set it aside and get on with life. But tonight, I'd let myself have a few hours with the road in front of me and the freedom to let that hurt.

So I rode through the night chill, hoping the open air would give me some answer on how I was going to set this shit aside.

I hadn't found that, not yet, when I stumbled onto something else.

The car on the shoulder caught my attention right off. It was late, and we weren't on a particularly busy street. At first glance, I thought it might be a cop hanging out. There'd been a couple drag racing incidents on this stretch —which I wouldn't deny the Disciples might have occasionally had a hand in. A patrol out wouldn't be a shock. It could be an annoyance for me, seeing as I was going well above the limit. But as I checked my speed, I caught a better look and saw the hood was up. It could be the owner just left the car there waiting for a tow and forgot to close the hood. But as I watched, I saw what I suspected. There was someone in the car.

Slowing further, I pulled off the road behind them. If they didn't have shit sorted already, I might be able to give them a hand either getting the thing running, or at least setting up a tow. The club owned the only garage in Hoffman. If folks wanted their ride serviced by someone else, they had to head into one of the neighboring towns. Should the problem here be something that required a tow instead of a quick fix I could lend a hand with, I could get that squared away for them.

I didn't have high hopes for it being quick. The Grand Am hadn't exactly been in production for a while, and the blue one I was looking at definitely wasn't a late model even at that.

When I got up alongside the driver's door, I saw it was a blonde woman behind the wheel. Her head was down, her hair falling all around her face. Hoping I wasn't about to scare the shit out of her, I tapped on the window. Her head came up quickly, but not with the kind of shock that said she hadn't heard me come up on the bike.

Then, she turned to look my way and everything stopped.

Evie.

I actually forced myself to blink, to clear my vision and verify this wasn't me losing my fucking mind.

It wasn't.

Unless I was well and truly fucked in the head, she was actually sitting right there in front of me. The fact that she looked about as fucking shocked as I felt made me inclined to believe this shit was very real.

Her mouth moved, those lips I'd thought about too many damn times seeming to form my name before she reached to open the door. It took all of the little remaining wits I had to get myself out of the way as she did.

"Evie," I rasped.

"Um…hi," she said as she got out and stood, her head tilted back a bit to meet my gaze.

So fucking close. She was right there in front of me. If I took one step, I'd have her pressed against me. And just that had my blood flow shifting in a way that I didn't need while standing on the side of the road.

That thought got my head together at least a bit.

"Are you all right?" I demanded.

Her brow bunched. "What?"

"Are you all right?" I repeated but got only that confused look back. It was cute. It was so fucking cute that I was damn close to losing track of what the fuck was happening here again. "Evie, you're stopped on the side of the road. Could be that's just car trouble. I'm asking you to confirm that's all it is by telling me if you're okay."

She blinked a few times before nodding. "I'm okay. I'm fine. My car just…" Her hand came out listlessly to indicate the obvious.

Her car just broke down on the side of the road at what had to be nearly midnight. A car she was in alone. That shit was not safe or all right, but that was beside the point at that moment. At least she wasn't hurt or anything.

"Good. Now, what happened?"

She sighed, and it highlighted the way her shoulders were slumped. I wished it wasn't so fucking dark and I could get a better look at her face, but maybe it was for the best that I couldn't.

"I don't know. I was driving, and it started making this weird sound. At first, I just hoped it would be fine, but then it kept getting louder. I pulled off to see what would happen if I turned it off. Apparently, that wasn't the right call because now I can't get it to start again."

It wasn't much to go on. Actually, it made me think this was probably a whole mess that I had no hope of patching up for her with no supplies.

"You got a flashlight on your phone?"

She nodded, fishing her cell out and turning it on. I walked to the hood while she held the light up for me to see. With little light and the shadows it was casting, it wasn't an ideal way to get a look. I checked the easy fixes to see if I could just get her on the road for now, but things seemed in order.

"Give me the phone, then I want you to go try to start it. Need to see what's happening when you do."

She obliged, climbing back into the driver's seat. It was hardly worth it since the whole fucking thing was too overheated to get a better look at. The engine didn't catch no matter how close she got to flooding it.

"All right, kill it," I called before lowering the hood.

Evie got out of the car again, taking her phone back as I approached. Her attention went to the now covered engine. "I don't think you shutting that is a good sign."

"Sorry, Evie. Can't say for sure what's wrong without getting a better look, but I know you aren't going to be able to drive off in it for now. Gonna have to get it towed."

Her head dropped, and it tore me up how defeated she looked in that pose. I gave her a second, waiting to see if she just needed to absorb that blow before bouncing back. She didn't. She stayed exactly as she was, and that worried me more.

"I can call, get that set up. One of the guys from our shop will come pick it up, then we'll take a look at it. Make sure you get a good deal and it's done right," I offered.

She still didn't move. That feeling of concern was rising into something that made my stomach turn. Evie hadn't been a part of my life in much of a real way, but what there was had been for a good spread of time. Never, even when she was clearly exhausted, did she let that light in her dim. It was part of what made her so fucking intoxicating.

Now, there wasn't even a flicker.

"Evie, babe, look at me," I urged.

She didn't. She did finally respond, though. "Do you guys have some kind of payment plan or something?"

Shit.

The fact that she was asking that when we didn't even know what would need to be done wasn't a good sign. That she was doing so and still wouldn't look at me was worse.

I couldn't say we did any payment plans at the garage. It was too slippery a slope when dealing with the sort of total-overhaul restorations we did there. If we agreed to terms like that, fixed up someone's ride, and they went back on the deal, we'd be fucked. You couldn't

27

just undo that work, and it would take more man hours to even try, but the cars weren't ours—not always, at least.

However, I could say we'd be able to set one up for Evie. Or I could, at least. Fuck, I'd pay the damn bill myself and work it out with her later.

"We can figure something out."

She didn't react to that, either. Not that I was expecting her to jump for joy about it, but there wasn't even an indication she heard me.

"I can give you a ride home for now," I forged ahead. "Lock the car, then I'll take the keys so one of the guys can come pick it up tomorrow."

Nothing. Not a fucking thing in response. My gut was in a vise. What the fuck was going on here?

"Evie," I called, firmer. Her head lifted a bit, but not enough to look up at me. "Babe, it's the middle of the night. We're on the side of the road, and you're still in your work uniform," I pointed out. "Gotta get you home. Yeah?"

She moved then, her head swinging around to look at my Harley parked behind her car. When she looked back, her focus settled straight ahead on my chest.

"I've got it."

"You've got it?" I wasn't following.

"I'll just call a cab or something. But I'll be fine."

Yeah, no. Not fucking happening.

"Right here, Evie. I can take you home. Fuck, I can

come by tomorrow and give you a ride to work if you need it, or the garage once we know what's up with your car."

"You don't have to." Her voice was firm like we were arguing and she needed to make a point.

"Do you hear me bitching about having to drop you off? You were anyone else, I'd advise you to call a cab. Might wait out here with a woman until they got here, but that'd be all. I'm offering because I know you, you mean something to me."

Her lips tipped in a way that looked a lot more like a grimace than a smile.

"No, I don't. Not really."

Fuck me.

"Evie, there's a lot I could explain there. Fuck, so much it's amazing you recognize me. The shit that's gone down since the last time I walked out of that diner makes me feel like I've aged ten years. But I didn't stop coming back because of our conversation the last time."

I wasn't sure if that was a lie or not. I'd told myself the last time I walked away from her that it would be for good, but the way the memory of her stayed with me since that day, I doubt I could have held on if there hadn't been walls, locks, and a shitload of guards making it true.

I couldn't look at her while admitting that to myself. If I hadn't gone away, I'd have probably been back at that counter in no time and then...

The old debate that was about to come back up at that train of thought came to an abrupt halt in my head.

The back of her car was stuffed full. There was even a box in the passenger seat. It looked like she was moving, even if the size of the car meant she couldn't be hauling all that much. Still, there was no other explanation for filling it that tight with suitcases and boxes.

"You moving?"

She blinked before rushing out a "what?" that seemed to be about buying time as it was a genuine request to repeat myself.

"Car's loaded up. Are you in the middle of moving?"

"Um… yeah."

Well, that shit wasn't convincing at all.

Not liking the cageyness, I pressed.

"I can call a buddy of mine. Just left him not long ago so I know he's up and not busy. He's got a truck we can load your stuff into, take it to your new place. Not exactly safe to leave it here with the car all night." I wasn't exactly sure who I'd call. A few of the brothers had rides that would do the trick. But it wasn't a lie, either. One of them would answer and haul ass out here to help me out.

Her eyes flared, panic in them, and I knew I had her.

"I…um…I…"

I cut off her stammering to ask, point blank, "Evie, where are you staying tonight?"

CHAPTER 4

Evie

WHY DID it have to be Stone that found me?

Why did he have to be so nice even after I made things awkward enough for him to disappear—something I knew happened regardless of what he said—over a year ago?

Why did he have to be so darn observant?

I tried to think up a lie quickly—a skill I was not particularly gifted at—and said, "I was—"

But he didn't give me a chance to stumble over whatever story I would invent because he cut me off with a firm, "Don't feed me a line of shit."

Well, that was rude.

"That was rude."

"You were about to lie your ass off and we both know it."

I mean, he wasn't wrong, but still.

"It was still rude."

"It's rude to avoid people's questions. I'm not exactly Ms.-fuckin'-manners, but probably more rude to make someone stand outside in the middle of the night hearing it

31

instead of giving them the truth so we can stop hanging out on the side of the road."

Since I'd been raised by a veritable Ms. Manners herself, I could say pretty assuredly he was also not wrong about that. Not that my mother ever covered this specific situation in any of her diatribes about proper etiquette, but I could assume.

I was tempted to point out again that he was still being rude, but that was obviously not getting me anywhere. Stone was a biker. Heck, around this area, he was the *head* biker unless something had changed since I last saw him. On that thought, my eyes dropped to the patches on his chest that read "Stone" and "President," verifying my assumption that he was still in charge. Perhaps it was fair to assume that manners weren't the paramount of the biker lifestyle. Maybe, in a situation like this, getting answers was more important.

With a sigh, I decided to stop fighting. "I was going to find a motel."

"A motel," he parroted.

"Preferably, a cheap one."

"A cheap motel."

Was he just going to keep quasi-repeating what I said?

"Yes. I need a place to stay, but I can't blow a bunch of money right now, so—"

"Why do you need a place to stay?" he cut me off, again.

And, just to say, the fact that he kept doing that was also rude.

"I just had an issue with my apartment," I evaded.

He didn't even bother with a response. He just looked at me like he was contemplating whether I needed a psychological evaluation.

For the first time since he stopped, lights shone around him with an oncoming car in the other lane. I watched as it passed, even keeping my eyes trained on it as the taillights grew distant. It really hit me again with that sight that we were still on the side of the road. In the time since my car broke down, only two people had even passed. The second didn't even stop. Granted, that might have been because Stone was standing there, looking markedly frustrated with me.

If only that look made him any less gorgeous.

I sighed.

"Evie, you gotta talk to me here," he pressed.

"I got evicted," I admitted. Then, because the wave of embarrassment at saying that overwhelmed me more than I anticipated, I continued, "It wasn't my fault. No, that's not right. It was. But it wasn't me that didn't pay the rent. I have been. My roommate didn't, and she hid all the notices. So tonight it was just…too late. And then I had to clean out my savings just to get my stuff out, so I can't even look for a new place until I get paid again, or maybe even a couple times."

After I managed to cap the verbal vomit, I looked up at Stone whose face was like thunder.

"Let's go."

"What?"

He stepped around me, leaned into the car for my keys, then slammed the door shut. Without a word, he grabbed my wrist and started pulling me toward his motorcycle.

"What are you doing?"

"Getting you out of here," he groused.

Oh, okay then. That was good. At least once he got me to a motel, I could go to sleep and call this day over.

"But what about my stuff?"

He stopped beside the front end, turning around to look at me. "Can't take it right now on the bike, but I'll come back for it."

"Wow. That's really nice of you."

Which was incredible and just more evidence that my life sucked. He'd always been nice when he came into the diner, it was part of why I'd developed such a huge crush on him. Now, he was proving that I'd only scratched the surface. After he'd turned me down, I didn't need this to prove exactly why that torch I'd been carrying for him hadn't ever gone out.

"Not a problem. We get back to the house, I've got a truck there. I'll come back here to get your stuff while you settle in."

Wait…what?

"I'm sorry?"

"We'll go back to my place. You can relax because, honey, you look dead on your fuckin' feet. I'll get in the truck, come here, and get your shit."

I was dead on my feet, absolutely. I'd been dead on my feet hours ago when I'd gotten back to my former apartment. Now, I was something even passed that. However, that was not the part of his previous statement that I wasn't understanding.

"Your place?"

His brows rose a touch, and I knew he was with me.

"Yeah. My place," he confirmed but did not elaborate.

Maybe I'd recolored the memories I had of him over the last year, but I didn't remember him being so impossible.

"That's not necessary," I declined, not certain how I would even handle being in his house with him. Especially not under the current circumstances. "I really just need to find a motel. Preferably a decent one, so long as the price isn't too high. Do you know any?"

His hand came up to rub at his eyes like I was exasperating him. I had to bite back the urge to scoff at the action since I was not the one here acting ridiculous.

"You aren't staying at a fuckin' motel."

Oh, no. Nope. I was not going to be ordered around. I'd had enough of that in my life.

"I am," I insisted.

He leveled me with a stare that communicated much more clearly that he was getting frustrated, but I held his gaze unflinchingly. He wasn't the only one here getting ticked.

"All right, I'll lay this out for you," he started, and I opened my mouth to cut in—despite the fact that it was rude, because I wasn't sure I cared anymore—but he spoke before I could, and louder to make a point that he wasn't going to let me. "You're a woman, alone, and fucking gorgeous to boot. You're small, and I'm thinking I'm not wrong in my guess that you could barely take down someone your own size, let alone a grown man with fifty pounds or more on you. I'm also thinking it's a safe bet that you don't have shit on you or in that car to help you in that effort. No weapons, no taser, or even fuckin' pepper spray—which, babe, you really should fuckin' have. I know every inch of this fucking town, and I can tell you there are four motels. Every one of those is a place you do not need to be in at all, much less when you've got no way to fucking look out for yourself if things went wrong. Further, even a cheap motel is going to cost money. You're dropping that every night to stay there, plus eating out because none of those places is going to have a kitchen, it's going to take you a fuck of a lot longer to get the cash together to put a deposit down on a new apartment.

"So I'm offering you a better option. I got a place for you to stay. It's not even mine if that really makes you feel better. The house belongs to the whole club, and it's big. I'm also not the only one staying there. Got at least one of the other brothers living there, plus a woman a couple years older than you and her five-year-old son. Then there's another brother and his woman that go back and forth between her place and the house. Even with that, we've got rooms no one is using, and one of those can be yours for a bit. It's not cool you got screwed by your roommate. It fuckin' sucks that you're in this shit situation when you were doing everything you were supposed to just because you trusted the wrong person. Way I see it, me finding you and having space to offer is the good karma I know you got coming to you. You just have to stop getting in your own way and accept it."

He was right about all of it.

I'd been worried myself about what sort of place any motel that would fit in my budget would be. I might have grown up sheltered in a lot of ways, but I wasn't an idiot. I knew the kind of things that went on at seedy motels. If I ended up in a situation, he was right in his estimation that I had no means to get out of it.

He was also right in his point about saving my money. And he hadn't even really gone for the gusto and pointed out the other financial burden sitting right behind me. When my next paycheck came in, it might be enough for a deposit on an apartment if I could find one in my price range, but it wouldn't be enough to also pay the first month's rent. Particularly not with carving it up bit by bit to pay for a motel room. But I would be hard-pressed to even earn another paycheck after that if I didn't get my car fixed. Hoffman didn't have much of a bus system to rely on.

I could do it all, and I would if I had to. I'd have to scrape out every penny I could, maybe ask around for more hours at the diner, but I could make it happen. Still, there was no denying that it would happen much easier and much faster if I took him up on his offer.

Doing so might be putting my heart on the line, but I'd just have to set that aside.

I focused on Stone, on his rough, handsome face that was not even marred a bit by the irritation it held as he waited for me to respond—and probably braced for more argument.

Then, even though the shame still clawed at me, I said, "Thank you."

He took me in for a beat, reading all that was in that gratitude, seeing that I was accepting his overly generous offer, and his lips tipped up slightly. Then, one of his hands came up. I noticed—as I had before when he came to the diner—how large it was before it moved from my line of sight to hook around the back of my neck. Before I could process what he was doing or react, he pulled me toward him a bit and leaned down to press a kiss on the crown of my head.

The simple affection of it choked me up. I couldn't recall the last time someone had treated me that way. It had been years. And coming from Stone, it was all the better.

"Come on," he said, holding out that hand to me, "let's get you home."

And I knew, with just that, that I was already in trouble. I should have been more focused on steeling myself from the minute I saw him. I should have had the wherewithal to maintain that guard when he touched me, but I hadn't. Now, it was too late. Not just because he was so passionate about helping, not because of the kiss. No, it was the way he said "home" like I might finally have one. It was the way my heart foolishly wanted that more than I could put into words, and it wanted it with him.

Oh, yes. I was absolutely in trouble.

CHAPTER 5
Stone

I WAS in big fucking trouble.

One day out of that cell, and I'd already managed to fuck myself.

If I hadn't known it the minute I saw Evie's face, I knew it feeling her pressed against my back on my bike.

Every biker I knew had his own philosophy about what that position meant. For some, any piece of ass he tapped or might want to was fair game to climb on behind him. Others were a bit more picky but still put their fair share of women in that seat. I wasn't one of those. Most of the Disciples had a different code. To us, no woman straddled your bike unless she at the fucking least had your respect. For me, it was even more. That spot was sacred. I'd never put a woman there.

A few times over the years, I'd had one of the brother's kids there. When I'd been a recruit and first got my patch, Cami and Ash had just been kids hanging around the clubhouse with their dads. Now, they were both grown, raising their own biker brats with my brothers, but there'd been times back in the day where both of them and Sketch —whose uncle had been one of us until we lost him in an accident years back—had gone for a ride with me. I'd even had Emmy out a couple times before I went away.

But I'd never had a woman on it with me. Not even once.

Now, the first woman I had ride with me was one who'd never even been on a bike. Fuck, Evie had just looked adorably confused about how she was supposed to get on even as I walked her through it. It'd taken all I had not to turn around and kiss her while she'd inched closer to me bit by bit, not getting in tight enough to keep her secure. I'd had to give in and grab her behind the knees to pull her close, then physically wrap her arms around me.

I'd never felt anything better than having her there.

I wouldn't even let my mind imagine how much fucking greater it would be to have her wrapped around me like that another way. It had been hard enough to keep some amount of control feeling her legs in my hands. If I lost anymore, we'd be eating pavement.

The next few weeks were going to be a constant battle with my self-control as it was. Moving Evie in was probably the dumbest fucking thing I'd ever done. I'd told myself again and again that I wasn't going to go to the diner looking for her. It'd been so long since I'd disappeared on her, it was best to just let it lie. Now, I'd be bringing her into my life.

I was so fucked.

As I stewed on that thought, I turned onto the long driveway that led to the farmhouse. The property had been left by one of our former presidents of the club. Back then, it had been the clubhouse. Now, we had the main clubhouse in town so we'd be close to everything, and this on the outskirts for whatever brothers or family that wanted to stay there to live in. It was sitting on sixty acres that was the picture of freedom. We didn't do shit with the land except mow a bit right around the house. The rest was left to grow as it would, unmarred because we paid out the ass on taxes to keep it that way.

I felt Evie finally lift her face from where it was pressed against my back to block the wind and knew she was looking around in the dark at the natural beauty of it. The moon had broken through the clouds enough to provide some light, but even with just my headlight, it was easy to see how different this was from the rest of Hoffman where it was tricky to even get half an acre to yourself.

Up ahead, the house was lit all around the outside. It wasn't some grand, fancy shit. It was a home. It was big, and it had needed to be plenty of times, but it was just an old farmhouse that we all took care of. I felt Evie's arms tighten around me as we got close, and I knew she was taking it in. I wondered what she thought of it. Was it a place she could see herself for the long haul?

Fuck. That didn't matter.

Once she was on her feet again, she was off to live her life. She'd never be back here.

I pulled up in front, killing the engine before saying, "Go ahead and climb off but be careful. The pipes get hot."

I felt her body jostle a bit with her nod before she did just that, stepping wide enough that I almost laughed. When I followed her, I found she was standing in the same spot, anxiously wringing her hands as her eyes moved between me and the house.

"I'll show you in and get you set up in a room, then head out to grab your stuff," I said as I led her to the door.

"Oh, I can come with you," she offered.

"You're going to go in and relax," I insisted. "Grab a shower or bath if you want. Fuck, you can go right to bed and get some sleep. I'll bring your stuff in and we can sort it out tomorrow. I can find something for you to change into."

"A shower sounds good," she admitted, and I watched her nose scrunch up. Fuck if it wasn't the cutest thing I'd seen in a long damn time.

I led her through the front door, stopping in the foyer to let her take off her shoes and the jacket she had on, then started the informal tour.

"Kitchen is right there. Help yourself to whatever you want. We don't do any of that labeling your food shit or anything. Everyone just does their part to restock things.

Never been an issue. And don't hesitate with any baked goods lying around. It's not anyone's. Daz's woman owns that bakery, Sugar's Dream. Kate, who lives here with her son, works there, too. From what I hear, the two of them just bring stuff back here all the time."

"From what you hear?" she asked.

So she caught that. The conversation was going to have to happen at some point. If Evie was going to stay here and be around the club, I had to tell her the ugly truth.

Mentally preparing myself for shit to go sour, I turned to her.

"Remember I said a lot of shit has gone down for me since I last saw you?" I waited a moment while she nodded, then another while I braced. "Truth is, not long after that last time, one of the brothers got into some trouble. It's a long story, but the gist of it is that he felt he had to take a particular course of action to defend someone he loves, and that course of action meant a man got the shit beat out of him. Unfortunately, instead of taking that shit that he'd earned, the guy got the police involved."

I paused again, Evie's attention rapt on me. "Fuck, I'm just stalling. Point is, I went to prison for the last year and a half. Just got released this morning. I guess it doesn't really matter why. What I want you to understand from telling you in complete honesty that I didn't do it is that you're safe. I'd never fucking hurt you, and neither would any of the men in my club. I confessed to that shit because it would have been worse for my brother if he'd gone away, but also because I supported what he did. His course of action might not have been right in most people's eyes, but he was defending his family.

"That's why I never came back to the diner. To tell you the truth, I walked away that day thinking it might be best if I didn't come back, but I would have. I know it because I sat in that cell thinking about how much I wished I could. It's also why there's a lot of shit around here that I don't know about besides what I've heard from other people."

I stopped there, realizing I was going way too fucking far and wishing I could take half that shit back. I didn't need to tell her how much I ached for her, not when there was no chance in hell I'd go there. It would kill me every day she was here, and probably for a long time after, but she wasn't mine.

"That's..." she swallowed. I was readying myself for whatever might come next. It could be she'd be afraid of me, of the Disciples, now even though I told her she was safe. It could be she was about to freak out and demand I take her somewhere else or call a cab so she wouldn't have to be alone with me anymore. If she did, I decided I'd let her. I'd give her some money—or maybe make Jager, who could hack damn near anything, "magically" transfer some into her accounts—and let her be on her way.

Then, she fucking floored me.

"That's incredible." Her voice was awed, and I didn't even know what to do with it.

"What?" I rasped.

"You sacrificed over a year of your life for your friend. I don't...I can't even fathom how hard that must have been for you." She stepped in closer to me, grabbing my hand like she knew I was a fucking mess and needed an anchor.

I was speechless.

Then, she destroyed me.

Hesitantly, slow enough that I could have easily stopped her if I had a lick of self-control, she moved in the last inch until her body was only just not touching mine. Without loosening her grip on my hand, she rose to her toes and kissed me.

Just that, a gentle, light kiss, broke any restraint I had left. In a moment, I had her backed against a wall, both my arms wrapped around her. Her hands came up to my neck, holding on tight while I damn near fucked her mouth with my own.

She was sweeter than anything I'd ever tasted. I fucking knew she would be, and still, the reality of it blew me away. I was hard as a rock, my dick desperate to get free from behind the zipper of my jeans, and still, I didn't even try to take it further. Not just because Evie was too good for that, but because kissing her was all I needed. I was sure in that moment that I could be sustained on just that for the rest of my fucking life.

And then she moaned.

That noise, the soft plea of it, hit me like a surge of heat but left pure ice in its wake.

This wasn't fair. I knew she'd had a thing for me before, and it seemed that wasn't entirely gone. I still couldn't go there, though. Not with Evie. Not with a sweet, beautiful girl too young to get caught up with a now ex-con biker too damn close to twice her age.

It physically hurt, but I forced myself to pull away. It took a second for her eyes to open and focus on me, albeit hazily. When they did, I stepped back.

She blinked herself into clarity, and I saw the hurt start to show before she hid it. I did that. I should have maintained the distance between us even when she tried not to, but I failed. So that hurt was all on me.

"We can't," I said, my voice hoarse.

"Right," she mumbled, no longer looking at me.

I'd fucked up, badly.

"I'm sorry. So fucking sorry, Evie. But you gotta know I'm trying to look out for you here."

"Right," she repeated. Nothing I was saying was even penetrating, and maybe that was for the better. Maybe what we both needed was for her to want nothing to do with me.

"I'll show you your room, go get your stuff."

Her head shook a bit, and I knew it was accompanied by a bunch of shit in her head that just wasn't true. Shit like I didn't want her, like she was a fool. I wanted to take those thoughts away, but I'd done enough damage as it was.

Instead, I led her to a room as far from mine as I could manage. After searching my own for some clothes that might manage to even stay up on her small frame, I told her where to find towels, and I left her to it.

Then, I drove out to get her stuff, all the while cursing myself for being a fucking idiot.

CHAPTER 6

Evie

I WOKE in the morning feeling confused.

This wasn't my bed. It couldn't be. It was too comfortable.

It was only then that my mind caught up enough to remember that I didn't have my bed anymore. The cheap mattress I'd gotten when I moved in was still sitting in the apartment unless it was in a dumpster behind the building instead. I'd wanted to take it with me and avoid having to find another halfway decent one for cheap, but there was no way to load that up in my little car.

I guess I needed to add "get furniture" to my to-do list before I moved again.

Another red line item in a budget that was in shambles.

Feeling a little unsure of what to do in this house that wasn't mine, I found myself pacing around the room. It was a nice space, nicer than I would have guessed for a bunch of bikers. Though, everything I had seen of the house last night—not that that was very much—was. This place seemed like a home. I half-expected an older woman who screamed "mom" from a mile away to come in ushering me out of bed and down for breakfast.

At the thought of breakfast, my stomach growled.

Had last night not turned into a disaster of epic proportions, part of the agenda for the evening before allowing myself to crawl into bed would have been scrounging up something to eat. Now, I was going on a full day since I scarfed down a granola bar on the way out the door.

With no car and barely any money, it wasn't like I could go out to grab myself something, so I was going to have to take Stone's word that anything in the kitchen was fair game. As soon as I could, I'd do my part to restock.

Unfortunately, there was more than concern about whose food I would be eating that kept me hiding in the room he'd installed me in. Because that was what I was doing, without a doubt. I was hiding, and I was doing it to avoid crossing paths with Stone.

I'd kissed him.

What was I thinking?

Well, that was a ridiculous question. I wasn't thinking. I was caught up in him helping me, and him talking about how he'd done so much more to help his friend that got into trouble. Not to mention, there was his gorgeous, rough, bearded face that seemed to be designed to bring my attention to his lips.

I really thought I'd learned my lesson with how it felt when he rejected me at the diner. The first time I'd ever gone after a guy, and he'd shut me down and disappeared. Granted, he at least in part explained the disappearing thing last night. I'd still had to experience it, assuming he'd just been run off by me asking him out.

How after going through that, my treasonous body had decided going for the gusto by kissing him was a good idea, I was certain I didn't know.

I did know that being rejected after physically throwing yourself at a man hurt a heck of a lot more than having one not want to go to dinner with you.

So much more.

Which was where the avoidance tactic came in. Clearly, I couldn't be trusted not to humiliate myself repeatedly in his presence. The only solution was to limit that circumstance as much as possible. Even if all I wanted was to be around him and have that easy friendship we'd developed before I screwed it all up.

My stomach made its discontent known again, louder this time. It was like I could hear it saying "stop being a chicken and feed me already" in that rumble.

Okay. There was nothing for it.

I found the sweatpants Stone had given me the night before and pulled them on, securing the drawstring waist as tight as I could get it. I had slept just in the t-shirt he'd brought in since the pants were large enough that I feared I'd just spend the whole night getting tangled up in them. Now, they'd have to do until I figured out where Stone had put my things.

After a pit stop in the bathroom where I wished for my toothbrush as I used some mouthwash, I retraced my path from the night before to the kitchen. The voices coming from it hit me just before the smell of dough and cinnamon. The noise my stomach made that time had me cringing, fearing whoever was in there talking heard it. Luck seemed to be on my side that morning, at least, as the conversation kept flowing.

It was an effort to not creep down the hall toward the kitchen opening, to not peek into the room before I made my entrance so I'd know what I was getting into. The only thing that stopped me was envisioning how awkward it would be if I was caught trying to be sneaky.

"Sugar, you're gonna have to cool it with this shit. He's a grown ass man; he isn't going to want to be coddled by a woman who's fucking younger than he is," I heard a male voice say as I approached. It wasn't Stone. Funny how I wasn't sure if that was relief I was feeling or not.

"You shut your mouth, boy. She can show up here whenever the fuck she wants and bake shit like this," another man, this one sounding older, responded. "You don't let this asshole tell you different."

There was a feminine laugh in response just as I turned the corner. The woman laughing caught my attention first, and I wasn't sure if anyone could have reacted another way. She was stunning. Even in a simple t-shirt and jeans, she looked like she should be stretched out on the hood of a car—or a motorcycle, I suppose—on the cover of a magazine. Her long, red hair was so eye-catching, it was a wonder I even noticed how…endowed she was. At least, it seemed a wonder to me. Somehow, I doubted men had any trouble noticing those features.

I hadn't even managed to look around to see who else was in the room before her laughter cut off and she focused on me. There was immediate confusion in her expression. It seemed Stone had not shared the news that there was a new house guest.

Unsure what to say, I moved my attention to the two men standing with her. I was right that one was older. If I had to guess, I'd put him in his sixties. His hair was all gray and there were wrinkles on his face that indicated he lived his life without fixating on such things. The guy beside him, however, gave the impression right away that he knew exactly how attractive he was. His grin screamed it, even though it didn't seem to be a conscious action. Both men were wearing vests like Stone's, which meant they were in the MC, too.

"Um… hi," I offered to the room.

There was a moment where I got no reaction from them, and then the younger guy gave a bark of laughter that made me jump.

"Well, looks like the pres went out and got himself some after all."

My face burned hot even as I watched the redhead take a few steps toward him and swing out an arm to whack him in the gut.

"Don't be a dick," she snapped.

He didn't hesitate to pull her against him. When she was where he obviously wanted her, he replied with, "You like my dick."

"Christ. I don't know what the fuck you see in him," the older man muttered to her.

Even as I tried to quell the burning embarrassment his comment caused, I could see precisely what she saw in him. He might smile suggestively by nature and make inappropriate comments, but he was looking at her like she hung the moon. I still wasn't sure about him, but that look said a lot.

I stayed where I was, transfixed by the sight of the couple together until the older man spoke again. "Well, come in, girlie. I'm Doc, the pretty one is Avery, and the asshole who needs to learn to keep his trap shut is Daz."

I did as he bid, stepping fully into the room, though not quite approaching them, as I replied, "Nice to meet you. My name is Genevieve, but most people call me Evie."

Avery extracted herself from her man's hold, aiming a smile my way. "You're just in time. I've got scones about to come out of the oven."

Oh, okay. "You own Sugar's Dream," I voiced the realization as it came to me.

"That's me," she confirmed.

"Stone mentioned you last night." I bit my lip after the words were out. It sounded like a confirmation that exactly what Daz had assumed had happened the night before.

But there was hardly a way to hide the fact that I had been there overnight.

"I wanted to pop over here and make him something good for breakfast since he just…"

She trailed off, and I realized it was because she was afraid she'd said too much.

"I know about him being in prison," I offered to ease her mind.

Her answering smile was tight with what appeared to be guilt. Taking in Daz, I saw his own grin was gone, and I understood. Daz was the one who'd gotten into trouble, and it had been for the woman he clearly loved. The burn in my chest that I'd felt when Stone told me what he'd done came back full force.

Avery forced herself to shake off the weight that had settled over the room first. "Well, I wanted to be sure he got something good for breakfast. Can you go wake him up? I don't want him to miss out on it being fresh and hot."

Right, they still all thought I'd just come from his bed. Jeez, that was awkward.

"I…um…. Well, I actually don't know which room is his," I shared.

The confused looks leveled at me did not help loosen my tongue to explain why I was there. None of them seemed quite sure what to make of me, and I was struck mute as a church mouse.

The awkward moment was broken by heavy footfalls and a rough, "Fuck, that smells good."

Stone came into the kitchen behind me, shirt rumpled and obviously having just woken up. I was relieved to see that he'd at least had the wherewithal to don a pair of jeans that I was guessing he hadn't gone to sleep in. I was going to have to be wary of that. I wasn't sure what the typical dress code was for the common areas of the house. Hopefully, being fully covered where it counted was part of it.

"Mornin'," Doc greeted.

I watched as Stone jutted out his chin in the man's direction, but his eyes were on me.

"Sleep okay?" he asked, his voice low. It may have just been that he wasn't fully awake yet, but I sensed it was an effort to wade in cautiously.

"Fine," I answered, making an effort to convey that in my tone as well.

He eyed me, but made the wise decision to move on and not cause either one of us to make a scene with an audience.

Noting the moment had passed, Avery chimed in with, "Breakfast?"

"Yeah," Stone affirmed, then turned to Daz and Doc. "After, could use a hand getting Evie's stuff in. Not much, but rather it be quick so she can get settled."

Doc turned to me with a warm smile, and I made the decision that I liked him. "So, you're sticking around for a bit?"

"Yes."

"Good. Always a good thing to raise the pretty ratio around this place."

Oh, yes. I definitely liked Doc.

I smiled at him and felt Stone's eyes on me as I did. It took all my focus, but I managed to keep from looking at him. It was a feat I achieved even as Avery served up the scones, and we all ate standing around the kitchen.

It was only when the guys filed out that I allowed myself to look his way and watched him walk away once again.

CHAPTER 7

Evie

"OH, THIS IS GOOD," Avery said once the guys were out of earshot. "The girls are going to love this."

"The girls?"

She got busy replacing the detritus of her baking into the proper cabinets as she said, "You'll learn that the club is a tight-knit group. When you belong to one of these guys, you become part of the group, and you get a whole chick posse by default."

I thought we'd cleared up the assumption that Stone and I were together with the whole not-knowing-where-his-bedroom-was thing. Apparently not.

"Oh, no. We're not—"

"Clearly," she cut in. "Stone might have more capacity for patience than some of these guys, but even he isn't going to install his woman in the house but let her sleep in another room."

"But you just said…" I trailed off because I was not keeping up.

"You're not his. Not yet, anyway. But, babe, you sure as shit still are."

That time, I just blinked at her. I couldn't say I was particularly experienced with men in general, and definitely not men like Stone, but what she was saying made no sense to me at all.

"These guys, the Disciples, they aren't like most men. But trust me when I say I know a lot about men, and no man brings a woman to his place and moves her in for no reason."

"I ended up in a bit of a situation. Stone's just helping me until I can sort everything out," I explained.

"Yeah, he's doing that. But he also could have given you some petty cash and been on his way. Hell, I'm guessing he could have not helped at all. Am I right?" She didn't wait for a confirmation on that. "Instead, he brought you here and is currently moving you in. I don't know why he isn't pulling the macho-man idiot stuff these guys like to and '*staking his claim*,'" she said that last with air quotes and a roll of her eyes before going on, "but I know you're still his."

"I'm not."

She opened her mouth to continue the debate, but I took a page from Stone's handbook and spoke first.

"Really. We aren't. I knew Stone before he went away. And I liked him. A lot," I admitted, my head lowering, the mortification still strong. "I asked him out, and he turned me down. I didn't see him again until last night. My car broke down while I was driving around to find a motel, and he found me. He offered for me to stay here, but it was just because he's a nice guy. That's it, and I know it because..." I took a deep breath, deciding this woman I just met was going to be privy to all my humiliation for some reason. "Because last night I kissed him, and he shut me down."

"Shit," she muttered.

It wasn't the word I would have used, but I couldn't deny the effectiveness. I just nodded my head in agreement.

"I don't mean to pick at the wound," she said in a gentle voice, "but did he stop you when you leaned in?"

"No."

She eyed me, then pressed, "So he kissed you back?"

He did a little more than that. I could still feel where his hands gripped me as he pushed me against the wall. I could feel every second of his lips and tongue taking mine.

With a cough to clear my tight throat, I answered, "Yes." There was a flicker of light in her eyes that I knew was trouble, so I went on, "But he's been in prison for a long time. I don't think it was so much me as it was just any woman."

I'd come to that realization as I'd laid in bed the night before, overthinking every moment since I saw Stone through my car window. He was a man that was probably used to having a woman whenever he wanted until recently. Now that he'd had his freedom restored, it made sense he would be eager to have that need satisfied.

Pushing that depressing chain of thought down again, I

proceeded. "You seem really nice, so I really don't want this to sound harsh, but I can't hear any of that. He's made it clear where he stands, and I need to let go and move on. But if you and 'the girls' want to hang out and talk about anything else, I'd love that. I just found out that the closest thing to a best friend that I had actually kind of sucked, so being welcomed to the fold sounds amazing. Just no Stone. Please?"

Without hesitation, she stated, "You got it."

I loosened a breath and felt some of the tension in my body relax. She wasn't angry or upset. That was good.

"I'll set something up with the group so you can meet everyone."

"That sounds great."

And it did. It might not have been smart to build a group of friends that was so closely entwined with Stone, but I'd find a way to make it work.

"All right, let's go upstairs and see what we can do with your room," Avery said, already bustling out of the kitchen.

I followed, feeling grateful that even though my life had fallen to pieces yesterday, I was already finding the silver lining.

LATE THAT EVENING, I was on the back deck with my textbook spread out in front of me. My life had gotten crazy in the last twenty-four hours, but that wasn't going to keep the tests from coming. I was two weeks from finals, and then I'd be finished. If I passed these last exams and logged the last few clinical hours, I would have my bachelor's degree in nursing.

I'd been certified as a registered nurse with my associate's for a year, but I had immediately enrolled in a program to get my bachelor's. I had hoped that I'd be working as a nurse by now, but unfortunately, none of the applications I had submitted bore fruit.

Until yesterday, I'd convinced myself that this might be a blessing in disguise. My job at the diner was not great, but at least the hours were steady. A nursing job might mean working nights that could be difficult with my schoolwork. Now, I was pining for the pay increase that even a starting job with my RN license would provide over my less-than-minimum-wage pay at the diner, particularly when the tips usually just weren't great.

I wouldn't let myself dwell on any of that, though. The finish line was right in front of me. After years of wanting nothing more than to achieve this goal, I could finally taste it. Soon, I'd be able to live out my dream of being a neonatal intensive care nurse.

"Still in school, then?"

I bit down on the inside of my cheek at his question. Perhaps I had underestimated how hard it would be to share a house with Stone. Tracking the sound of his steps as he approached, I gave myself a mental pep talk.

You can handle this. You've faced far worse than an unrequited crush. Time to toughen up.

"Just one last round of finals," I replied.

Stone knew all about my plans. I'd still been working on my associate's when we met, but I knew then what I would do when I finished. He'd listened to the whole plan, and he'd been the first person not to question if it was the right one.

"You know what you want, you know how to get it, and you're making it happen. That's fucking great, Evie."

"Does that mean you have graduation coming up?"

It was a logical question, but it felt foreign to me. The surprise of it made me look up at him.

"No. This part is all online. There's a graduation I could attend if I really wanted to in Seattle, but I already stated I wouldn't be walking," I explained.

He'd meant to make small talk, but that was out the window. His attention was fixed on me, his brow furrowed. "Why would you do that?"

"Why travel all the way to Seattle for it?" I countered. "It would be one thing if I was going with a bunch of family to watch, but I'd drive all that way just to walk across that stage alone."

"You can't say you're going now?"

"I don't know. Probably not. It's too close now."

"Find out," he ordered.

What?

When I didn't hop to doing that, he repeated, "Go on wherever you have to and find out if you can still walk."

His tone brokered no argument. This was the president of a motorcycle club, the man who had to be firm enough to lead a group of men most people would never question. Yet, I couldn't help but do just that.

"Why?"

"You worked your ass off for this, you deserve to be there."

"Stone…"

"And if you don't want to go alone, then I'll take you."

Where his command had failed, that managed to silence me because it was too much. It didn't say helping someone you knew out when they hit hard times. He was talking about traveling hours away to celebrate a pivotal moment in my life, the kind of event that family went to, the kind of event you attended for someone that you loved.

My mind a mess of words I wanted to say, my gaze fixed on the books spread out in front of me. Soundlessly, I closed them and stacked them up. Only once that was done, only when I'd had a minute to get some semblance of order to my mind, did I look back to Stone, who'd watched every movement.

"Thank you," I started and saw that catch him off guard. "You've done a lot for me, and I don't think I'll ever be able to repay you. But you don't have to do this. I don't want you to. The ceremony isn't important to me, but if it was, I wouldn't want to be there with someone who just went because they felt bad that I'd be there alone."

Stone was going to butt in, I could see it. Since it had worked earlier with Avery, I sallied forth before he could.

"You're really sweet, and I appreciate it that you want me to have that, but we both know how I feel about you. I'm sorry that I'm making this complicated, but those feelings are still there for me even though I know they aren't for you. So you being at something like that for me, it would only make this more difficult."

Knowing I couldn't withstand much more, I went to grab my things and get out of there.

I didn't get the chance.

Before I could so much as turn away from him, Stone had my wrist in an iron grip.

"You seriously fucking think I don't feel that shit?"

His face looked like it was made from pure fire, and it silenced any words I might have drawn up.

"You think I sat on that stool every fucking day you were there to stand there smiling across from me just for the food? Because I'll tell you right now, I didn't even fucking taste that shit. I was there for something I needed a fuck of a lot more than food. I was there to see that cute smile on your perfect fucking face."

I wasn't smiling then. Even though his words were

exactly what I wanted to hear, the harsh way he said them scared me.

"I told you that day you offered me that invitation to get everything I'd been wanting for months, and I told you again last night, I'm trying to do what's best for you. Now, I'll give it to you even more straight. You're twenty-seven. I'm forty-four. You're beautiful and smart; you're sweeter than any woman I've ever fucking met. I'm the president of a fucking MC. I'm a fucking convict. And you know I didn't earn that time, but I've done plenty of shit that could have gotten me the same rap sheet. I'm too fucking old and too dirty to even think about having you, but I do. I thought about it for eighteen fucking months sitting in that cell, and probably the only thing that kept me sane was picturing your face. But you've got your whole fucking life ahead of you, and I'm not going to stain that."

He stepped closer to me, one hand coming up to run callus-roughened fingers down my cheek.

"I'm not for you, even if it fucking kills me to admit it. But one day when you find the man that is, you'll be glad I did. And I'll still probably be wishing that man was me."

Before I could begin to process all he'd said, before I could say even one word to stop him, he turned away and left.

CHAPTER 8

Stone

"SO, EVIE," Daz said, leaning in my open office door.

I was at the clubhouse, the morning after walking away from Evie. I'd spent most of the night before drowning myself in whiskey, like that was going to do a damn thing for me.

Now, the brothers were converging for church—our club meetings. It was time to step back into my role as president of this club. A couple of the guys had questioned the call. They thought I should take a little time to enjoy my freedom before getting back to it. I'd fed them a line about the club not being a burden. Not that I thought it was, just that it wasn't my reason for getting down to it. No, my reason was trying to keep myself distracted.

I'd been doing a halfway decent job before Daz came sauntering up like an asshole and ruining it.

"What do you want?"

"She seems sweet. Like toothache sweet," he persisted.

I leveled him with a look not a lot of men would fuck with. Daz, however, was either stupid or had balls the size of cantaloupes. He claimed the latter, but there was a fuck of a lot of evidence of the former working against him.

Instead of taking the warning, he came in further and planted his ass in one of the chairs across from me. He went so far as to lean back and put his feet up on the edge of my desk.

"Respect. Personally, I went with easy for my first taste of freedom." Yeah, I remembered Daz's coming home party. If memory served, he'd gotten at least a few tastes of easy that night, closing it out with two in his bed at the same time. "But I can see the appeal of going that route."

"Get your fuckin' feet off my desk."

He did, but he looked no more ready to get out of my face about this.

Before he could keep at his nosy shit, I asked, "Are you in here for a reason?"

Apparently, his hearing worked better than his sight because he at least caught my tone.

"Brothers are all here," he answered.

"Good." I got to my feet, getting the key from my desk drawer that unlocked the room we used for church. "Let's go then."

I didn't wait for him. I walked out of my office and into the lounge where the club was all hanging around waiting. Even the recruit, Hook—or Dustin before we gave him the road name for the mean right hook he had as one of Jager's boys from the gym and fight circuit witnessed—was there even though he wouldn't be allowed in.

Behind me, as he always did, Daz bellowed out, "Time for church, you fuckin' heathens!"

Doc was already at the door, collecting phones. I tossed him mine before I went for the lock. Not like anyone would be calling me. Damn near everyone that might was following behind me. Evie wouldn't call even if she had my number.

I paused at that thought, wondering if I should give it to her. Maybe talk to Daz and get Avery to pass it on. Except that would bring that fucker even more into my business. No, it was just going to make things more tense if I tried to get her my number now.

Shaking that off, I took up my seat at the head of the table. The room wasn't huge, but it was big enough for the long table we'd bought custom to seat the whole club around it. The walls were covered in Disciples' history, and our patch—a bike and two scythes—was painted on the wall.

I watched my brothers file in, taking their usual spots. This felt like it could have been just weeks since the last time we'd been there. Nothing here had changed.

On the table in front of me was the gavel one of the brothers had gotten for me years ago when I first became president. I had no idea who did it. The thing had just been sitting on my desk one day. Even in all the time that had passed, no one had owned up to it. Now, it stayed in that same spot at all times.

Roadrunner, my VP, grabbed a seat next to me. He'd

been holding down the fort around here while I was inside. He'd also made a point to keep me appraised of anything and everything that had been going on, bringing it all to me before taking it to the club. He'd taken it all on even while Ember, his daughter and Jager's woman, was pregnant and then giving him a grandchild just a few weeks back.

"Never could bring myself to use that thing," he said, eyes on the gavel where mine had been. "Didn't feel right."

I couldn't help but think maybe, after him handling shit around here for over a year, it should be his now. Maybe my time at the helm was supposed to be up.

Without thinking about that too long, I took up that wood handle and brought it down twice. No one spoke, waiting for me. A shit ton of things were on the tip of my tongue, but I went right to business.

"Roadrunner, you're up," I announced.

"Gotta talk about the prospect," he started with. "Boy's been wearing that patch too long. Our pres is back, time to right that."

I waited for him to call the vote, but he didn't. It was my job to do so, and he was stepping firmly back into his role as VP. It was a statement, to me and to the club as a whole.

"All in favor?" I asked.

A round of ayes met me, not one person thinking Hook hadn't earned his spot. I'd told them more than once to give him his patch while I was inside, but apparently, even he'd said it wasn't right. That went a long way to cementing my respect for him beyond what I got to know before.

"We got a patch for him yet?" I asked.

"Got it," Jager answered. Since he brought the kid into the fold, it was his responsibility.

"Someone go bring his ass in here, then," I ordered.

Ham got up first, opening the door wide and yelling, "Yo, Hook. Get in here."

It took not even a minute for him to do as ordered. That was life as a prospect. You did what you had to, paid your dues. No doubt the brothers had eased up on him since he'd been stuck a prospect longer than anyone, but that didn't mean defying a direct order.

When he stepped through, Ham snapped the door shut behind him. Even as he did, Gauge was on his feet getting a chair from the corner to add to the table as the brothers shifted to make room.

"Your party, you pick a night. When you do, we have a party and you get your patch. For now, you're a brother by vote, so you need to be in here for this," I told him.

He didn't say anything, just gave a jerk of his chin and took his seat. Regardless, there was a shift to his posture that said it all. He was proud to have that place, and that meant fucking everything.

"You got a night in mind?" Slick asked. His woman, Deni, usually took charge of getting shit together for the parties. She'd need to know.

"Want to wait a bit. Next month, probably. Got a fight coming up that isn't going to be an easy win. I need to focus."

"We'll get it set after, then. Yeah?"

He didn't waste words there either, just gave a nod.

"Good. Next up," I moved us on, turning back to Roadrunner.

"The Devils. Whatever the fuck they have going on up there, it's past time to take a good hard look. Been hearing a lot of rumors about shit quality ice and girls in bad shape. It might not be our business, but those rumors are circling closer and closer to Hoffman."

Shit.

The Devil's Horror motorcycle club was a bunch of fucking thugs who used the title of being an MC just to make themselves more intimidating. They were a biker gang, not a fucking club. There wasn't an ounce of brotherhood behind that patch, and that ill will was a lot more bitter for anyone that didn't wear it. Roadrunner had been keeping me apprised of that situation for a while. Up until recently, those assholes seemed to know their place and stick to their turf. Over the last few months, they'd been making moves.

"I gotta connect with Andrews either way," I started. "I'll see if he's got anything for us. If those dirty sons of bitches are approaching Hoffman, he's going to want us prepared to put an end to that either way. Jager, when you've got the time, want you poking around whatever you can find from them. They aren't the most organized bunch, so I'm not expecting they'll have some master plan you can hack, but anything you can get might help."

Jager jutted out his chin. If there was anything to find, he'd get it. The man could hack damn near anything.

With that, Roadrunner moved on, going over the latest updates from the garage—which he ran with Gauge's woman, Cami's, help in the office—followed by Jager giving updates about his gym and the upcoming fight schedule—sanctioned and underground—and Daz filling us in on business from the strip club.

By the time I banged that gavel again, calling it to an end, it was easy to forget that I'd been gone. This, stepping back into my role in the club, my place in this life, was easy.

I was on the way out when Gauge stopped me.

"Got the status for you on that Grand Am," he said, an eyebrow up.

Yeah, it wasn't our usual bread and butter. Savage Restorations specialized in just that—restorations. The garage had cars and bikes from around the northwest coming in to be redone because our guys did great work. We also worked as a full-service garage, though.

"What's the damage?"

"Not too bad. Had to replace the regulator, but that's all to get it running again. The thing's in decent shape for what it is. Obviously taken care of. Still, it's going to start having problems. Could do a whole lot of preventive work, but it's going to outpace the value of that car."

I was tempted to have him fix up every issue he could find, just to know it was going to be safe for her, but I stopped myself. She was finishing school. She'd get a job soon that would hopefully afford her the ability to trade up. And, most importantly, she would not thank me for overstepping.

"Just leave it at the regulator unless something else is pressing. And get someone to drive it out to the farmhouse when you can."

Gauge, being smart enough to know not to push me unlike Daz, didn't question it. "Got it, Pres."

Well, if nothing else, her car would be running again. It wasn't much, but I could give her that.

CHAPTER 9
Stone

TWO WEEKS.

Two fucking weeks Evie had been living in the farmhouse, which should have been like a dream made real.

Instead, it was a goddamn nightmare.

Since that night I'd laid it out for her, I hadn't been back.

I hadn't seen her even once since I left her standing on the porch.

And I was fucking miserable.

Every night since that first, I'd been staying in my room at the clubhouse. There was one big, glaring issue with that I hadn't thought of: every fucking person knew. It wasn't uncommon for me to be around the clubhouse more often than not, but crashing there that many nights drew attention.

It didn't fucking help that Evie being around wasn't a secret. By the time we'd had our confrontation on the back porch that night, the whole club probably knew about her, and they were making their assumptions.

The fucked part of that was, their assumptions probably weren't wrong.

All this meant I was trying to avoid everyone, even while I spent all my time at the clubhouse where it was impossible to be alone.

Like I said, fucking miserable.

The knock on my office door didn't help improve my sunny disposition any.

"Yeah," I called.

Roadrunner sauntered in and took a seat. He didn't hesitate, didn't ask for permission. It wasn't often any of the brothers would. Formalities and shit like that only pissed me off.

When he didn't launch right in, I went ahead. "You know, you've earned some time off the clock. Go hang out with your girl and your granddaughter."

"Love that little one to pieces. She's got every part of my heart that doesn't belong to her mother, and she will until they put me in the ground. But, shit, my baby having a baby makes me feel old as fuck. I spend too much time there, I think they'll age me to the point I can't get my ass on a bike anymore."

Bullshit.

"Ember kicked your ass out," I guessed.

"No. Jager did. The motherfucker said I was hogging Jamie," he grumbled.

I laughed just picturing the two of them squaring off over the baby. They'd gone toe-to-toe a time or two over

Ember, but I figured this was going to be even worse. Jager had always been a surly asshole, and we'd all been shocked when he fell hard and fierce for Ember. Now, none of us were surprised he took protective to a new level with his daughter.

"Anyway, I sat through an interesting conversation while I was over there. Thought I'd come give you the lowdown," he informed me.

Where he was going with this, I couldn't begin to guess.

"I don't even want to think of what means she used to do it," Roadrunner went on, face set in a sneer at the thought. "But Ember talked him into getting on his computer and find out when Evie finishes her exams since she's being cagey and the girls weren't liking that."

None of that was a surprise. Not Jager hacking into something because Ember wanted him to, not the girls going to whatever lengths to bring Evie into the fold.

"And?" I didn't bother trying to act aloof. I'd known Roadrunner for two decades. He'd see through that shit either way.

"They decided she needs to go out and celebrate."

Shit.

"Do I want to know what the fuck that's gonna entail? Or should I just call Andrews now?" Andrews was our in at the Hoffman PD. He took care of us the best he could. If the women were talking about going out as a group— especially if Ham's old lady, Max, was involved—he might be needed.

"They want to take her out to get drunk. Since none of their men are feeling great about that happening somewhere they can't control, Avery offered up Candy Shop as a spot."

God fucking help me.

"They want to take her to a fucking strip club?"

"Tomorrow's dick day," he reminded me.

Candy Shop had been around Hoffman for a while, but it only belonged to the club the last couple years. That investment was Daz's brainchild and his responsibility. From the last reports Roadrunner gave me, the place was making crazy turnover, so he was right to pull for it. What none of us expected when he suggested it was that a big part of that success would be the money they made on the third Thursday of every month when the whole night was dudes up on the stages.

"Christ."

"Could be worse. Ember mentioned Avery was all about taking her out somewhere she could meet a man at first."

"And I thought she liked me," I muttered despite myself.

Roadrunner's brows shot up at my poorly veiled admission in that.

"There's an easy way to put a stop to that," he pointed out, fishing.

"Not happening," I pronounced.

He didn't push, but leaned back in his chair, settling in and making a statement all the same.

"That age gap? It's about the same as you and Ember. Tell me, if Jager wasn't in the picture, would you want some asshole your age going after your daughter?"

His lips pursed. "Catch your point. But it ain't easy for me to picture any man with her, and that includes Jager even two years later. Is that what you're worried about? Her family?"

Leaning an elbow on the desk, I dropped my head into my hand. Going around and around this was giving me a constant migraine.

"No. Not specifically. I knew her for months before I went inside, and she never mentioned them. The girl was working in a rundown diner for years while she put herself through school, and not direct out of high school, either. If there's any family there, I'm not thinking they'd be a high priority to impress.

"But it's still that shit. It's the fact that every time I went out anywhere with her, people would be looking at us and wondering what the fuck is wrong with her that she's with a man old enough to be her father. It's the fact that she's still young and should be experiencing that with someone her age."

"Well, shit. I didn't realize you were some stuffy civilian who gave a shit what people thought and stayed cooped up inside not living your life," he shot back.

"It's not about me. It's about her. She's a sweet girl, too

fucking sweet to put up with that shit just because she tied herself to a man like me."

Roadrunner sat forward, one hand braced on the arm of his chair, ready to stand. The other came up to tap twice on the desk between us as he said, "Didn't realize our president thought so little of this life."

"You know I fucking don't." I lived for this goddamn club. How the fuck he could accuse otherwise after all I'd given…

"You think she had cause to be ashamed to be at your side says differently."

With that parting line that hit right on target, he got up and walked out. Meanwhile, I was left wondering if I was making a huge fucking mistake.

CHAPTER 10
Evie

I LOOKED at the computer screen again, just taking it in. There they were, my final grades. With that, I'd completed my bachelor's degree. It almost didn't seem real.

Years later, finally having achieved the goal I'd gone after even in the face of losing everything of the life I'd known before, I hardly felt like the same girl who'd meekly accepted her parents' plans for her.

"IN JESUS' name, we pray. Amen."

Father finished saying grace, but I sat still in my seat. Mother and I were to wait until he first filled his plate before we did the same. I always wondered why he took so long to do so. Perhaps he was not often hungry.

I was starving. Mother felt I'd been putting on some weight, so she'd decided it was best I cut out full lunches. Instead, I'd had only a few carrot and celery sticks that day. I knew it was wrong, but I had daydreamed of more food with each bite.

If Mother or Father had known I was having such thoughts, I would have been lectured again on how gluttony was the easiest of sins to fall victim to. They had told me again and again how easy it was to let our sinful thoughts convince us we were hungry when we needed nothing.

Maybe they were right, but my stomach had ached all afternoon. It felt like real hunger.

"How is your schoolwork, Genevieve?" Father asked, and I was glad I heard him. Unless he had deviated from his usual routine of first asking Mother how her day had been, I had not been listening. It was rude to do so, especially when being spoken to. Neither of them would have been pleased if I had not responded when he asked.

"Very good."

I was homeschooled, though Mother did not teach me. Father and many of his parishioners worried about undue influences in the schools, so the church funded private schooling during the day for us. Mr. Jennings taught all of us, despite our ages, so it was largely silent reading of materials provided for our grade level.

"You had an exam today if I remember correctly." I knew Father had my school schedule in his office so that he could ask after tests and projects.

"Yes, in science. Mr. Jennings already reviewed my answers and gave me top marks."

Father pursed his lips, though he said nothing as he finished piling some green beans onto his plate. He then passed the bowl to Mother as it was time for us to start serving ourselves. He dug in without waiting, as usual. Though, there was still a tension about him. I knew it was because of the mention of science.

Father did not agree with the state mandates on what we were required to learn in that particular subject. He said we were being taught mistruths that flew in the face of God. I would never say it to him, but I wasn't sure that was true. From what I learned, it seemed that our understanding of science was a gift He gave us.

"Is that all that happened today?" He moved away from the uncomfortable subject.

"Mr. Jennings also talked with me about the PSAT exam I need to take soon."

Another purse of his lips. "Yes, he mentioned that to me as well."

"He said it was important to consider what my plans might be in the future. He said there are private universities that are committed to the Lord that I might consider if that was my path. I think I might like to learn more about that." I forced myself to stop and take a breath as the nerves rose up. Father hated when I stuttered or said um, something I did often if I was not careful. "I think I might like to become a nurse."

It was immediately clear that this was the wrong thing to say. Mother froze with a slice of roast suspended over her plate. Father swallowed the bite of food he was chewing and deliberately set his fork down. His attention fixed fully on me, and I squeezed my hands together in my lap.

Then, he simply returned to his food while saying, "That won't be an issue. Your place is not at a university. It is here. Your duty is to our flock."

Oh, okay.

I bit down on the inside of my cheek. It was disrespectful to question one's elders, but I was not sure I understood. When I figured out a good way to say it, I released the hold to a metallic tang, and spoke.

"Of course. Our service to the Lord must always come first. How do you see me doing my part for Him?"

I had thought becoming a nurse might be that path. I had not said it, but I wanted to do so at a hospital and work with infants. Surely, seeing to the health of babies was a righteous path.

"You will do as your mother does. You will be a pastor's wife and care for the things he is too encumbered by his work to see to. You will help him lead by example in living a pious life."

There was an unflinching finality to his tone that told me all I needed to know. This was not a discussion, and it was certainly not a debate. This was his will, and it would be done.

"Of course, Father."

THAT DAY, I'd buried my burgeoning dream of being a nurse down deep. I'd truly thought it would never be because I was born to a different life.

It would take years for me to see that my life was mine to make of it whatever I wanted.

Now, I had made a huge step toward doing just that.

And later that night, I was going to have my first night out with "the girls"—and by that, I meant any girls, not just this new group that was making an effort to make me feel welcome—to celebrate.

"SO, WHAT ARE YOU WEARING TONIGHT?"

Avery was sitting cross-legged on my bed. Her hair was styled perfectly straight and left loose to highlight the length of it and she had her makeup done, but she was still in a pair of yoga pants and a tattered hoodie that I would guess was Daz's by the size. She'd come in a minute ago, plopped herself down, and asked that question.

After I first met Steph, I wondered if moments like that were going to be what having a roommate was like. It hadn't been. Steph was the roommate that was usually closed up in her room, or else expected me to be if she moved out to the couch. We were friendly, but I would never have felt comfortable going into her space just to hang out or offer fashion advice.

I'd never had a friend like that. The closest I'd ever come was Mrs. Norton who lived around the corner when I was growing up. She was in her seventies, retired, and lived for her bridge nights—where she and her friends gambled, something my father liked to make a point of speaking against anytime her name came up. She was hardly best friend material for a teenager, but she had been a source of advice beyond the strict edicts my mother liked to recite.

"Um…I'm not sure." What did you wear to a strip club, even if it was guys dancing? "Am I supposed to dress up?"

Avery shrugged. "The crowd is usually mixed. Some people will just be in normal clothes, but there's a lot of bachelorette parties, girls' night outs, that kind of thing, so a lot of people will dress sexier."

My wardrobe had come a long way since it was all under my control, but I wasn't sure I had the means for "sexy" by most people's terms.

"What are you wearing?" I'd seen Avery a fair bit over the last two weeks. She was always dressed pretty normal.

"Well, I've never been in the crowd before. Even since I stopped working there, I've only been backstage with the guys. I figured for tonight I'd actually try. They'll get a kick out of it. So it's a little black dress and red pumps for me."

I definitely did not have anything in the little-black-dress category, but I wasn't focused on that anymore.

"You worked there?" My attempt to keep the shock out of my voice did not succeed. I wasn't certain how I was going to be able to get inside the doors. Working there seemed impossible.

"I didn't mention that? I worked there even before the club bought it. It was how Daz and I got together since he runs it now. Hell, I was the one that taught the guys everything they know."

Taught them…as in…

"You were a…um…"

Wait. Was that inappropriate to ask? Was 'stripper' a negative way to say it? Should I say dancer?

"Yeah, I was a stripper," she let me off the hook. "Sorry, I thought I mentioned that. I'm so used to everyone in the club knowing, I guess."

There wasn't shame there, and it made me feel a bit in awe of her. I could barely open my mouth without ending up embarrassed. She just owned it, and that was so cool.

"Evie?" she called after a moment. I focused on her, realizing I'd gone into my own head again.

"Is that why you're so good with makeup?"

She laughed, and there was a hint of relief to it like she'd been worried I was judging her. "Yeah, it was important to figure it out. I started in my first club at nineteen to get away from home. It didn't take me long to figure out the better I was with my hair and makeup, the more money I got. The more money I made, the less likely it was I'd ever have to go back, so I practiced until I was a pro."

I nodded along as she spoke. That I absolutely understood. "You did whatever you had to in order to get out."

Her expression changed to concerned and I realized I'd said too much. It wasn't like I was hiding my past, but I didn't want to open up those wounds tonight. In an effort to veer away from that topic, I asked, "Will you do my makeup? I haven't really figured that out."

When she replied, "Sure," I knew it was because she chose to drop it, not because I fooled her. Not Avery, who'd run away from whatever home she'd had, too. "Let's find you something to wear first."

It took some doing, but we finally settled on a lavender sundress I'd bought on a whim almost two years ago. It was the first dress I'd even tried on since I left home and was no longer forced to wear nothing but. In truth, I'd bought it after I'd known Stone for a while. It was around the time I started thinking about asking him out. The dress had been a part of a fantasy that he might say yes, and I would need something to wear on a date. Though I'd meant to wear it with a cardigan, something Avery zealously insisted was not necessary.

After she'd done my makeup and even took it on herself to fiddle with my hair a bit, adding some loose curls, I found she was right. The bare shoulders and deep —for me—scoop of the neck left me more exposed than I was used to, but it looked good.

An hour later, even after seeing Avery in her tight dress and heels I couldn't imagine maneuvering in, I still felt confident in it.

Daz's reaction as we left the house helped.

"It's a good fuckin' thing you aren't going out to some bar with a bunch of dudes around. This whole thing," he said, moving a finger back and forth to indicate Avery and me, "this angel and devil shit, you'd cause all kinds of trouble."

"You never know," Avery replied, moving to him and putting her hands on his chest, "we still might."

"I don't doubt it, sugar."

He took her lips, heedless of the red lipstick she had on before leading us out to his SUV.

It was time for girls' night.

CHAPTER 11

Evie

THERE WAS a guy on the stage. He was shirtless and wearing just a pair of dangerously low-slung sweatpants. At that moment, he was down on his knees, rolling his hips into the air.

Seeing that, I was torn between hiding behind my hands or breaking into nervous laughter.

Maybe both.

My confidence that I knew what I was getting into tonight took a severe hit.

Things had started off well.

It had been arranged that all of us girls would be driven to the club as well as have rides home. This was, according to Avery, so we could all feel free to drink, and because it helped avoid setting of the "over-protective asshole tendencies" their men apparently had.

Daz, Avery, and I picked up Ash, a pretty blonde with curly hair whose blousy top and well-fitting jeans made me feel a little better about how I'd dressed, and Ember, who looked right out of a pin-up photo in a skin-tight, off-the-shoulder top, a high-waist swing skirt, and heels of the

Avery, how-do-they-even-walk-in-those variety. Her hair was even done up with big curls and a black bandana tied like a headband.

As soon as she got in the car, leaving a rather scary-looking guy in the door watching her leave, Avery asked, "How the hell do you look like that two months after having a baby?"

Wait, this woman just had a baby? It wasn't possible.

"This skirt does wonders for covering the baby pooch," Ember explained.

"Or the fact that she's a kickboxing instructor and worked out nearly right up to the birth," Ash whispered conspiratorially to me.

After that, the conversation in the car seemed to all focus on me. Where I was from, asking about my nursing program, my plans now that I was finished, and how I met Stone. It didn't feel like an interrogation, and no one pressed when my answers about Stone were not overly forthcoming, so I was relaxed by the time we got to the club.

Once we were inside, that was a different story.

We'd met the rest of our group inside. Cami, Deni, Quinn, and Max rounded out a bevy of women that it was no wonder they caught the eye of a bunch of men like Stone. They were all gorgeous, and, like Ember and Avery at least, seemed to have a lot of attitude. Only Quinn and Ash seemed to be more on the quiet side like me.

Not even a minute after we were seated in a little area

marked VIP, Max—who I could tell right off from her exuberant greeting was loud by nature—demanded Quinn's phone to call her man, Ham. If Stone hadn't given me Biker 101 lessons when I'd asked about his name, I'd have been most confused about Ham's name of the guys I'd met. Since I knew road names could come from anywhere, I just went with it.

In trying to avoid watching the half-naked man and his *thrusting*, my eyes moved over the crowd of women raising drinks in the air and crying out jovially. It was why I noticed him first. Although, first only referred to the group I was with. Plenty of women around the room were noticing as he moved through it.

Though, it was a wonder if you could not notice him. He was huge. Standing at least a foot taller than me—but probably more—and built like some kind of mythical folk hero, he was garnering a whole lot of appreciation from the crowd.

It took a minute for me to realize he was striding right for our table with laser focus. Only once I caught on to that did I notice his cut.

So this was Ham.

Wow.

He honed right in on Max, seeming to stomp right up to her. Unless that was just the way he walked. I was inclined to believe it was stomping by the hard lines of his face.

"Hi, babe," Max chirped up at him, not even a hint of caution at his expression.

"You fuckin' owe me for this," he growled.

"What?" she asked, and even though we'd just met, I couldn't miss that the innocent tone she used was anything but.

"I gotta walk my ass in here with some dude up there putting on a show with his cock for a bunch of horny women that were ready to maul me just for walkin' by, you gotta pay up later."

"I need my phone," she argued.

"Yeah, and you'll be payin' extra for leaving it behind on purpose to make me do this shit just because it fuckin' amuses you."

"I don't know what you're talking about."

I was starting to think Max was a little bit crazy until Ham gave her a wolf's grin before leaning in to say something in her ear. Seeing that, I understood. This was a game, and they were both playing it.

Ham took his time at her ear, then moved down to her neck. That was my cue to look away. Desperate for something to watch that wasn't the show on the stage or the one being put on a few seats away from me, I grabbed a drink menu off the table. None of the words filtered through, but I kept my eyes on it until I heard Ham speaking full volume again.

"All right, I'm getting the fuck out of here. Gonna go the back way and avoid the cock-thirty cougar party."

Avery chimed in there with, "If you're trying to avoid the show, I might not recommend the back way. The guys aren't great about staying confined in the dressing room."

Ham glanced between the curtain beside the stage and the way he came before he said, "Surprised I made it through that mess with all my clothes in one piece. Not anxious to see any dicks, but it ain't nothing I don't have. I'll take my chances. Besides, your man's back there in the office?" Avery nodded. "Might pop in and try to knock some goddamn sense into him again. Fuckin' male strippers."

That earned him some laughs, but I was too caught up in the whole scenario to join in. As if he could sense I hadn't had the proper reaction, Ham's attention honed in on me.

"You're Evie?"

I nodded, and he grinned.

Wow.

Max was a lucky girl.

Ham looked to her and said, "He's so fucked."

What?

He focused back on me, saying, "You look like a good girl. Be careful with this one." His head jerked Max's way.

My eyes darted to her, then back. "She seems nice," I blurted.

He chuckled and muttered, "Totally fucked" as he did.

Weird.

Ham turned, leaned over Max, and said—still loud

enough for us all to hear—"Give me a kiss so I can get the fuck out of here, toots."

She obliged.

When they disconnected, he took off toward that curtained doorway. I saw Max watching as he went, her expression wistful. She loved him, and I was struck by how beautiful that was…

"Damn, he has a great ass," she announced.

Okay, so they had what seemed like a strange relationship to me, but what did I know?

Even with all the barbs they traded, I was certain I wasn't imagining the real emotion between them. And maybe the way they squared off was exactly the reason they fit. It was strange, but that made it even more beautiful.

Once he was gone, she turned her attention back to us to announce, "We should get some shots!"

I WAS SIPPING on my fourth drink—doing this so I wouldn't be yelled at by Max again for not drinking, but knowing I really needed to slow down—when a body plopped down on the couch next to me. My attention swung that way to see the sweatpants guy from the stage sitting next to me.

My mouth was hanging open, but he showed no reaction to that as he grinned and said, "Hi."

I didn't even have it in me to stumble out my umms. He was sitting there in a white t-shirt and jeans, his legs already up and resting on the low table in front of us. I wondered if any of the other women in the club noticed him there, but I was too afraid to look away for fear this was part of the show and he was going to get up at any second and start stripping right there.

"Don't worry, sweetheart. I'll keep my clothes on. Unless you don't want me to," the very attractive male stripper offered.

"Leave her alone, JJ," Avery called to him.

JJ, as he was apparently called, stuck out his lip in an exaggerated pout. Even making that face, he still looked like he could be in a movie playing the really gorgeous boy next door.

Well, if the boy next door took his clothes off in front of a room of cheering women, anyway.

"First you turn me down all the time, then you up and fucking leave, and now you're cockblocking me? What gives, Cherry Pie?" he complained.

"She's off limits," Avery shot back, unfazed.

JJ's eyes came to me, and even in the dark club, I could

tell they must be a brilliant blue. "You belong to a Disciple?" he asked with more than a hint of surprise.

"Um…no?"

"You don't sound too sure about that."

"I don't, but…" I managed to shut my big mouth before I blurted out the rest.

"But you want to," JJ supplied anyway.

Yes.

I didn't say it, but I could tell he read it in my face anyway.

He looked around the L-shaped couches we occupied. "Any of you not spoken for?"

A couple of the girls shook their heads at the same time Max announced, "I'm not."

Quinn rolled her eyes. "Yes, you are."

Cami laughed as she informed him, "She's Ham's so I would not go there."

JJ eyed Max. "You're gorgeous, babe, but I've seen that fucker. I like my face the way it is. Pays the bills, you know?"

"Fine," Max muttered, downing more of her drink. I was pretty sure it was her sixth, or maybe she was on seven now. At the very least, she'd been overruled on the shots idea. I'd never done a shot—not that I was going to say that with her around—but I was pretty sure it wouldn't end well. Then, she dropped her disgruntled attitude and perked back up to ask, "Do you sleep with women that come in here a lot?"

"Max!" Quinn reprimanded. It seemed like she did that or the eye rolling a lot when it came to Max. I'd learned that Max had been Quinn's best friend for years. When Quinn moved here to be with Ace, her husband, Max decided to come, too, and that was how she ended up with Ham.

"What? It's a valid question," Max argued.

Deni leaned toward me to share, "I'd settle in, she's just getting started."

So, I did. While Max asked JJ how much body oil he used, how he decided his costumes, if he could do the "Dirty Dancing" lift with her, as I sipped my drink. Without thinking it through, I drank the one the waitress replaced it with, too, until after the inquisition ended.

A while later when the waitress returned with a tray of shots to groans and Max's delighted laugh and order to "Drink up, bitches," I didn't protest.

I also learned that shots burned.

Still, I was having the most fun night I had ever had, so I enjoyed that burn as it settled into a heat in my chest. Girls' night was the best.

"Okay, one more," Max piped up after the empty shot glasses were taken away. "Do you accidentally hit yourself in the balls a lot?"

CHAPTER 12
Stone

MY PHONE CLATTERED on the nightstand.

At that hour, it was probably because something was going to shit.

Snatching it up, I didn't bother with the display. Whoever it was, I had to fucking answer.

"Yeah?"

"Heads up," I heard Daz through the line, "your girl's fucking smashed. All the women are." There was a scuffling on the line, then his voice directed to someone else, *"No, you aren't giving Max more fucking stripping lessons now. Sit your asses down."* I could hear the indistinct whine of women's voices in response before he came back to me. "Fuck, I fucking apologize to anyone that's had to corral my ass when I was this drunk."

"Last time I had that job, you passed out on the way home after screaming at me for not taking you to get tacos," I reminded him. It was still easier dealing with him, though. After he'd lost consciousness in the backseat, I left his ass in the car overnight.

"You didn't have eight of me," he argued. "At least Ham'll be here to get his crazy fucking woman off my hands."

I heard Max's *"hey!"* in the background.

"You sit down and stop harassing the guys, I wouldn't have to say it," Daz said to her.

"You guys getting them all home?" I asked.

"Yeah. That's why I'm callin'. If you aren't at the farmhouse, you should get on your bike."

Fuck. When did my club start turning into a bunch of assholes that got in everyone's business? "Brother—"

"Apparently, Evie likes to cuddle when she's plastered. Never seen anything like it. JJ went to sit with the girls after his last dance, and half an hour later she was nearly laying in his lap."

I was a fool, but that shit got me out of bed.

"Fuck," I muttered, looking for pants.

"She wasn't making a move. From what I've heard since I got out here, she won't shut up about you. But drunk Evie takes sweet to a new level. Not to mention, she's fucked. Seriously. Max got them doing shots at one point. Your girl's going to be a fucking mess in the morning —if she even makes it that long."

My decision had been made already, but that would have done it, too.

"I'll meet you there."

"Good call, brother."

I ended my call, found some pants and my cut, and got out the door.

I WAS on the front porch at the farmhouse when Daz pulled up. As soon as they were stopped, Avery was getting out of the passenger seat.

"Dammit, sugar. I told you to fuckin' wait. You're going to hurt yourself in those shoes," Daz snapped at her as he came around the hood.

For her part, Avery didn't look that drunk. She had a small smirk pulling at her lips, but she was steady on her feet even with the shoes.

"You've seen me dance in taller ones than this. I'm fine," she sassed back.

"One of you want to tell me where Evie is?" I demanded.

"She's in the back," Avery answered.

Seeing as I was looking in the backseat window and there was no head there, I looked to Daz.

"She fell asleep. We dropped Ember first, and she laid

down with her head on Ash's lap until she had to get out, too." He shook his head. "I'm telling you, she's something else. Mutterin' about how nice everyone is and how cool they are. Asking to babysit all the kids and have Ember and Avery give her a makeover."

"Which we're so fucking doing," Avery added.

Christ.

I went to the back door, looking through the window first to make sure she wasn't leaning against it. She wasn't. She was curled up in a ball across the bench seat, facing the seat back like she was snuggling up against it.

"Come on, sugar. Time to make this shit up to me," Daz said, and I heard his footsteps going toward the house.

"What about Evie?"

There was a pause, then a little shriek. I glanced over my shoulder to see Daz had slung her over his. "Stone's got her," he grunted as they went inside.

Yeah, I had her. She was right there in front of me again, and somehow in even just two weeks, I let myself forget the draw of her.

Pulling open the door, I watched her lie there without stirring for a minute debating what to do. I could try waking her, or just see if I was able to get her into bed without her stirring. The second option was the smart one.

"Evie."

She shifted around but didn't wake.

"Sweetheart, you gotta wake up."

The sleepy groan that time had my cock responding even more than it did to the dress she had on, and that dress with the way she was laying showed off nearly the whole length of her legs in a way that was fucking testing me.

Going for broke, I leaned into the truck, reaching out to brush her hair back. It was soft, so fucking soft just like I imagined all of her would be. She leaned into my touch, but even then, her eyes stayed closed.

Maybe there was some kind of higher power keeping me from making a mess of my life.

Slipping my arms beneath her legs and back, I hoisted her up. She'd never have been heavy, but after eighteen months of working out to pass the hours, I was in better shape than I had been since I left the Marines. Even getting her out of the car door was easy now.

When I had her out and the door kicked closed, I adjusted her so she was leaning on my chest, her head on my shoulder. My sweet Evie snuggled right in, face nuzzling into my neck.

I got about halfway up the stairs when the movement finally made her stir.

"Wha—"

"Sh. You're all right, sweetheart. Gonna get you to bed."

"Yours," she murmured.

"What?"

"Your bed. You're cozy." She nuzzled farther in like she was trying to burrow into me.

"Not sure that's a good idea."

Her head came out of my neck, and her hazy eyes settled on me. "It is. I know it."

"Evie," I started to argue, but she scrunched her face.

"No. I thought I should leave you alone, but Ember said she had to keep at Jager. She said sometimes you have to be willing to fight for what you want." Her words slurred a bit, but there was a deeper clarity to them that shocked me. "I'm small, and I'm not that strong, but I'm used to having to fight for what I want. I left my home to get it. I can fight. You'll see."

It came out like a threat, but some part of me that was already screwed wanted it to be a promise.

Her face relaxed, having made her point, but that fucking nose of hers twitched.

Fuck, but that got me every time.

"Okay, bunny. My bed."

"Okay."

So I did just that, taking her to my bed and laying her in it. She was already out again by the time I did. Without waking her, I stripped off her shoes. Her purse was nowhere to be seen. Hopefully, it was just on the floor of Daz's truck. If not, the crew at Candy Shop were all people Daz trusted, so they'd probably just stash it somewhere for safe keeping.

With that done, I got in beside her. I shouldn't have,

really fucking should not have for the sake of my own sanity, but I couldn't resist wrapping my arms around her and pulling her into my side. Even in sleep, she came willingly, wrapping an arm around my middle and a leg over one of mine.

I laid there for a long time thinking that I'd imagined that exact scenario a hundred times lying in my shitty cell bed. Sure, in my head I'd fucked her to exhaustion rather than her getting drunk off her ass, but it wasn't just the sex I'd thought about. I'd pictured this. The stillness, the quiet. My bed in the place I called home and a beautiful woman next to me.

Fuck, that imagining went back before I even knew Evie.

It went back to when I was younger than her, a rifleman a few months into my time with the Marines. My corporal decided we needed a few words before we shipped out for the first time.

"Every man that goes to war has to keep a picture in his mind. Something other than the blood and the gore. You don't have that, you aren't gonna make it through. That's the brass tacks. Being a Marine means we do what we do for our country, for freedom. I'd never diminish that. But when you're in the thick of it, when shells are falling, men are dying, and you feel like you haven't had a real night's sleep in a year, that ain't always goin' to cut it. Some of you will be leaving behind a woman that's got your heart. Some of you might have kids. You got all the motivation you need right there. Those that don't, I suggest you find something to hold onto. Something you've got,

something you want, doesn't matter. It just has to be something you can hold onto when you got nothing else."

I had no idea what I could keep in my head that'd see me through. I wasn't leaving behind anything. Mom had already passed. My dad was a fucking scumbag that ran out on her. I had no family. I didn't even have the club yet. But something about what he'd said about the guys that had a woman, a family, already having what they needed, stuck.

So when that time came, when the shit I was seeing in service to my country threatened to overwhelm me, the image I clung onto was a simple one. I imagined laying my head down at night in a real bed, away from all the shit we were mired in, living my life on my terms, and a soft, warm woman that had it all from me at my side.

When I left the Marines, I didn't let go of that image for a long time. Even when I found the club, when I took my place in it, I held onto that. It was only after years that it started to fade.

Until I met Evie.

Until they closed me in that cell and I was back in a place where I knew I needed to hold onto something to keep it together.

Only then, unlike when I was younger, it wasn't a vague, faceless woman. It was her. And that image was all the sweeter for it.

Right then, experiencing a part of that—even if it was one night and I'd never get it again—I felt content in a way

I never had unless I was on my Harley with the wind in my face.

I felt fucking free.

And I knew, no matter what I'd told myself, that there was no way I was letting go. From right then, in the dark, while she slept peacefully, Evie was mine.

CHAPTER 13
Evie

BEFORE I EVEN OPENED MY eyes, I felt it.

"It" being the pain in my head that felt like my brain was pounding against the inside of my skull, trying to get out. Instinctively, I knew taking that step was not going to be a good thing. The unfortunate truth of it was that lying there without looking was giving me time to notice all the other parts of me that seemed to be in an open state of revolt as well.

My stomach ached, but that didn't overshadow the nausea. My throat was sore, but the idea of even drinking water to ease it made me want to gag. I couldn't even start on how horrible the taste in my mouth was. On top of all that, my whole body simply ached.

In the years since I'd left home, I'd come to realize that a lot of the things my father had railed against in and out of his church were wrong. However, after last night, I might have to concede his point on alcohol.

It was devil juice. Pure and simple.

I started to groan, then cut off on a wince because even the sound of my own noise was too loud. The movement sent a sharper wave of nausea roiling through me.

God, I'm sincerely sorry for whatever I did to earn this. If you just make this stop, I promise to never drink again.

When my body relaxed back to just the latent misery I was saddled with this morning, I finally had the clarity to notice I was not laying in a bed. I had a blanket on and below me, wrapped around my back, but the surface beneath it was hard. And once I realized that, I noticed that the thing under my head wasn't a pillow. It was too firm. Still afraid of opening my eyes, I reached an arm up to feel what it was. It was rounded and long, and there was something rough covering it like…

Jeans.

It was a leg.

Oh, okay. Someone was there. That was…alarming.

Bracing for the agony I was sure was coming, I opened my eyes just enough to get a peek. At first, my vision was too blurred to make anything out, and then I noted it was dark. Or at least, dark enough that I wasn't blinded. Maybe it was still night. When I had enough of a handle on what I was seeing to take in more, I gingerly turned my head to look to my right.

Stone was sitting there, leaned against a wall, his eyes closed.

Oh, jeez.

Next to him was a tub, and I realized the hard thing I was laying on was the bathroom floor. Given the state of my stomach, it didn't take a genius to figure out why we were in there.

What surprised me was that I had no memory of getting there. Or of how Stone ended up there with me.

The last thing I recalled was being in the car on the way home. We'd shut down the club, hanging out until after the last dance had ended and the crowds were gone. Then, Daz and Ham practically pushed us all out the doors and into their cars, breaking up the hug fest as we all said goodbye to do so. I remembered being in the car was making me kind of dizzy, so when we dropped Ember off, I laid down in the little space she'd cleared up.

After that, it was all blank.

Definitely, after this, alcohol and I were not good friends.

And I was starting to have my questions about Max since she was the one that made me drink so much.

I let out another groan, this one quieter after learning my lesson.

In response, I saw Stone stir.

"You feelin' sick again, bunny?"

Bunny?

And why was he being so loud?

"Shhhh. Why are you shouting?"

He chuckled. It sounded so good, but it also made his leg move. It was probably barely anything, but it felt like the whole world was shaking beneath me.

"Please stop moving," I begged.

When he spoke again, he did it much softer. Though it still twinged a bit to hear, it was much better. "Tried to get you to bed after you stopped, or just give you a pillow. You just settled in on my leg."

Well, we could add the burn of humiliation onto the other symptoms I was experiencing. Of course, that triggered the delayed mortification of processing that he'd been in here while I'd been throwing up.

Never. Drinking. Again.

I shut my eyes, hoping I could at least stave off some of the physical pain if not the mental anguish. When I did, I felt Stone's hand sift through my hair. I barely contained my sigh at how good that felt. At least if I had to live knowing he'd seen me that low the night before, I got this as a consolation prize.

Honestly, it might be totally worth it.

Maybe I'd humiliate myself again. Stone always seemed to be around for those moments.

Oh, jeez, now I was just being dramatic.

"You ready to move to a bed now?" he asked, still running his fingers through my hair. "My back's had about all it can take."

Right. He'd been sitting up all night on the bathroom floor. "Sorry," I whispered, not only to keep my own voice down but also because the way he was playing with my hair was relaxing me to the point I was nearly asleep again.

"Do it again," he replied oddly. "Didn't like you being sick because I know firsthand how much that shit sucks, but you're a sweet drunk and get even more so when you aren't feelin' good."

Really, at this point, I didn't even want to know.

"Come on," he urged anyway, "let's get you up."

With his assistance, I managed to get up to a seated position with no small amount of misery. He stood and stretched while I seriously contemplated just laying back down. Standing didn't seem within the realm of possibilities.

As it turned out, it didn't have to be. Once he stretched his back, Stone leaned down not to help me up, but to pluck me right off the floor and carry me.

"What are you doing?" I demanded as he hoisted me up.

"Taking you to bed."

"You can't carry me," I shared.

"You think you walked from the car and up the stairs last night?" he shot back.

Not based on that question, I didn't.

"You carried me up the stairs?"

"You're light; it was easy."

Or he was just strong. Based on the muscles I could feel then and had seen already, I was thinking one of those was more likely.

He was about to step out of the bathroom when I cried out, "Wait!"

The word bounced around in my head, striking like a blow.

"Jesus, Evie. What's wrong?"

"I need to brush my teeth," I explained.

"You can't even stand."

Sure I could.

Maybe.

"I need to," I insisted.

With a sigh, he knelt until he could lean me forward and my feet were right on the floor. He didn't release my torso until he was sure I could stand on my own. Or at least until I stopped teetering so much.

"You good?" he asked.

"Mhm." Peachy. Totally. Legs were supposed to feel like Jell-O, right?

"You got it in you to take two steps to your right so I can find you a toothbrush?"

"Mhm," I answered, but didn't move. This was mostly because I was trying to figure out which way was right. When his hand came to my hip and applied pressure to one side, I figured that was a good bet and moved with it. Stone disappeared from my side, so it must have been right.

A thought occurred to me then. "Why do you need to find me a toothbrush? I have one."

"Not in the same bathroom you use," he explained. "This is an en-suite to my room."

Oh, okay.

I'd not only spent the night on a bathroom floor with

Stone after seemingly puking my guts up, I'd done all that on *his* bathroom floor.

It just kept getting worse.

After hunting around for a minute, he stood back up with a toothbrush in hand. He didn't give it to me, though. He turned on the tap, wet it, then got the toothpaste tube and squeezed some on the brush first. That was sweet because I wasn't sure how long all those simple tasks would have taken me.

"You're good at this," I told him.

"Using toothpaste?" he asked like I'd lost my mind.

"No," I responded as I took the brush, "taking care of me."

The room felt weird as I focused on getting through my task. I just didn't have it in me to figure out why.

When I'd finished with the brushing and rinsing business—which was more complicated than I ever remembered it being before—Stone asked, "You need to do anything else in here before you lay down?"

It was a pointed question that even I didn't miss.

Awkward, but also weirdly sweet.

"Yes."

"You gonna be able to handle that?" I got the sense that if I did say no, he'd actually stick around to at least help me get to the toilet.

Nope. No way. I'd die of shame if he did that.

"I've got it."

"You sure?" he pressed.

"Yes."

"All right," he said, moving to the door. Before he stepped through and closed it, he warned, "Gotta turn on the light. It's pitch black in here without it. You ready?"

No. I definitely was not.

I squinted my eyes, hoping that would stave off some of the light before I gave him the go ahead. Squinting, I found, may have helped, but it did not keep the light from making my head pound worse.

After, when I managed to wash my hands and get through the door, I found Stone sitting on the edge of his bed, waiting for me.

"I'll just…" I started but trailed off when he stood and came my way.

"Get in bed, Evie. We both need more sleep. You'll feel a fuck of a lot better later."

Well, yes. Sleep was my plan, but not in here.

"I can go back to my room," I said, gesturing vaguely to the door since I didn't know which way my room was from here.

"Babe," Stone replied like this was a response that made sense rather than just a word.

"What?"

He sighed and looked to the ceiling like he was seeking deliverance. "Just lie down. I'm fuckin' wiped."

Not having the capacity to put up a fight, and not able to resist the allure of getting into Stone's bed with him, I did as he asked. He walked around the bed, getting in the far side by the time I'd gotten to the close edge. I climbed in, the soft surface beneath me instantly stealing any alertness I had left.

I collapsed, not moving as Stone pulled the covers over me. I was already drifting off when he settled and then reached over to pull me into him.

Maybe I should have protested. Maybe, had I not been hungover and exhausted, I would have. Since I was those things, and because I really liked the feel of his big, warm body wrapped around mine, I didn't.

I just fell asleep.

CHAPTER 14

Evie

WHEN I WOKE AGAIN, it was to an empty bed.

The sharp pain that was triggered by trying to do anything earlier had mellowed into a dull ache. The nausea had subsided. What remained was a fair bit of dehydration.

I rolled my head to the side and noticed that Stone had already made a point to see to that. There was a glass of water on the bedside table. Beside it were two pills I assumed were ibuprofen.

After giving myself a few minutes to wake up, I downed both before getting out of bed. Since Stone hadn't come back, I decided to head to my own room and get some fresh clothes. I was still in the dress I'd worn last night. Frankly, I felt disgusting. I was a shower-every-single-day type of girl, and it had officially been too long since my last.

The moment I stepped into the hall, I realized where I was. That being that I was in the room adjacent to my own. Stone had put me right next door to him, and I hadn't even known. Realizing his space was so close only confirmed my suspicion that he hadn't been sleeping here. If he had, there was no way I would have gone so long without so much as seeing him.

I hustled to my room, then across the hall to the bathroom. The hot water felt incredible, like it was managing to wash away all the lingering effects of the alcohol in my system. I knew it was unlikely it'd still feel so good when I got out, which was why I found myself delaying and staying under the hot stream.

As I did, my mind wandered back to Stone. If he hadn't been here the last couple weeks, where had he been? My stomach tightened at the thought that he'd been in prison for more than a year. Men—and women, I was sure—had needs. He'd told me that night that he'd stumbled onto my broken down Grand Am that he'd been released the same morning. Maybe all those nights I didn't see him coming to his own bed meant he was in someone else's. Or multiple someones.

The thought had that sick feeling I thought I'd gotten rid of coming back with a vengeance.

It wasn't my place to feel that way. We weren't together. Actually, he'd made it quite clear that we were anything but. Still, it hurt to have those faceless women in my head.

When I was forced to admit that my minute of enjoying the shower had started turning into a way to avoid the possibility that Stone was still in the house somewhere, I forced myself to suck it up and get out. Getting ready afterward might have involved a few non-essential steps and a fair bit of lally-gagging, but I emerged from the bathroom not too long later ready to face whatever was waiting for me—even if what was waiting was a whole lot of nothing.

I poked my head in the open door of Stone's room first, checking to see if he'd returned in my absence, but there was no sign he had. Seeing that, I headed down the stairs. It was at the top of the steps that I got a whiff of the smell.

Bacon.

Funny how that smell both obliterated my trepidation and made my stomach turn. It was delicious and nauseating and appealing and sickening.

I was definitely not drinking again if that was going to threaten my relationship with bacon. Alcohol was not worth ruining a good thing like that.

Following that smell—and hoping there was extra if I could bring myself to eat it—led me to my primary goal. Stone was there in the kitchen alone, manning the stove.

Not sure what to say exactly, I cleared my throat.

His head shot up, eyes honing right in on me and a smile forming beneath the scruff of his beard. It just served to remind me of another thing that wasn't fair. Why did his beard have to be attractive? I'd never liked beards. I'd never liked anything that was Stone before him. True, I'd never liked any man all that much, but still. I'd always imagined I'd end up with a man that was cleaner cut. This was probably because I knew it was the only type of man my parents would approve of, so I'd narrowed out all other options subconsciously. Then, when I was free of their expectations, I'd found Stone and developed a taste all my own.

A taste that definitely included that beard.

"Heard you get in the shower, so I got this started," Stone said as a greeting. "Feelin' better?"

"A bit. Thank you for the ibuprofen."

"Midol," he corrected.

"I'm sorry?"

"Yeah, don't ask me. That shit works. Don't even remember who it was that shared that around the club or how they found out, just know nothin' works as well on a hangover."

I'd actually heard that before, and it made sense. Still, it was bizarre to hear a bunch of bikers kept a supply of Midol for any reason.

"Appreciate you holding back the laughter," Stone said as he flipped the bacon. "There's orange juice in the fridge. Glasses in the cabinet next to it. Good to get your blood sugar up, too."

I moved to do as instructed at the same time I commented, "You know all the tricks for a hangover, huh?"

"Had more than my fair share of wild nights, bunny."

Bunny.

I'd forgotten about that. He had called me that that morning.

I was about to ask when he spoke again. Even when he didn't know he was cutting me off he somehow managed to.

"You get that, you grab a seat. Food's done."

My stomach lurched, and I felt the grimace on my face. "Um…"

"I know," he answered my unspoken hesitation. "It sounds like the worst idea, but trust me. You gotta eat. You get some food in you, you'll feel a hell of a lot better."

Funny enough, beneath the worry, I did feel kind of hungry. As disgusting as it was to think of, I'd probably lost most anything I ate the night before. And now, it was…

"What time is it?" I asked, unable to see the oven or microwave clock around him.

And speaking of the time, I had no idea where my purse and phone were.

"Just after one," he answered, grabbing a plate.

Oh, okay. That was a bit alarming. I wasn't sure I had ever slept that late.

"Do you know where my stuff is?" I asked, focusing on things I could do anything about.

"Got your purse from Daz's car earlier. He took off with Avery to her place. It's on one of the chairs in the living room."

Well, that was good at least.

I was sitting at the little table off to one side of the

kitchen when he approached with two plates. One went down in front of me, the other across the table before the chair he pulled out for himself.

"Eat," he ordered.

There was a whole spread here. Bacon, eggs, a blueberry muffin, and home fries.

"You made all of this?"

"Not much to it," he replied. "Bacon and eggs go in a pan. Potatoes were from a package, already cut and shit. Just had to warm them up. Muffin is one of Avery's. Brought them here yesterday knowing you guys would probably tie one on."

Apparently, everyone had been prepared for that but me. I'd actually thought it was crazy we were getting chauffeured to and from the club. After the night we'd had, it was making much more sense.

"Well, thank you. It looks good anyway."

I started with the muffin. It seemed like the safest thing on the plate for my stomach that had quite a night and was in knots from sitting across from Stone. Once again, it was impossible not to see why Avery owned a bakery. She had a gift, there was no doubt.

"Now that the worst has passed, you have fun last night?" Stone asked.

That conversation was certainly a lot safer than any of the million questions I had bouncing around in my head.

"Yes. I don't think I'll ever want to drink again.

Certainly not that much. But the girls were really nice and fun."

"Good. They're a good group of women. It'd be good for you to get to know them."

Would it? I wasn't so sure. When I left this house, they'd just be a tie to Stone, an excuse I'd be able to use to keep him in my life in some way.

Stone went on, "And you don't have to swear off booze. I'm assuming you don't have much experience drinking?" I nodded in confirmation. "You get a handle on it. Or else you learn the times you drink with a good group like that are worth a bit of suffering the next day."

I felt ridiculous having him tell me that. I wasn't some nineteen-year-old kid. Heck, I was closer to thirty than I was to my twenty-first birthday—or younger—when a lot of people drank too much for the first time.

"Do you think I'm weird?" I asked for some unfathomable reason.

Stone looked about as confused as I felt. "Sorry?"

Well, there was no way out of it at that point. "I just… I'm twenty-seven, and last night was the first time I've ever been drunk."

"First time I got that drunk, I was fourteen," he shared.

My mouth dropped open. "Fourteen?"

He nodded. "You think that's weird?"

"At fourteen, the big development in my life was that I started looking after some of the younger kids at vacation Bible school."

Stone grinned and shared, "And, honey, that I definitely can't relate to. There's no weird or not. You never got drunk, it wouldn't be weird. It'd just be your life. So long as it's your own choices, you do whatever the fuck you want and it's no one's place to judge."

"That's very sweet," I told him.

"It's the truth, nothing more. But you want to think I'm sweet, I'm not gonna try to stop you."

Was he…flirting?

I couldn't ask that. Or could I?

Why couldn't I just have a normal dating experience like every other twenty-seven-year-old out there instead of fumbling around like an awkward teenager would?

I focused down on my breakfast—or was it lunch at this point? It felt like something had changed between us, but I was afraid to ask. The last two times I'd felt there was something there and acted on it, I'd been shown I was wrong.

"You seriously fucking think I don't feel that shit?"

"I was there for something I needed a fuck of a lot more than food. I was there to see that cute smile on your perfect fucking face."

"I told you that day you offered me that invitation to get everything I'd been wanting for months, and I told you again last night, I'm trying to do what's best for you."

"You're beautiful and smart; you're sweeter than any woman I've ever fucking met."

Those words he'd given me the last time I'd seen him

came rushing back. I remembered them all. They'd practically haunted me since he walked away that night.

No, I hadn't been wrong. He felt it, too. I was just gun shy now.

Then, a bit of the night before I'd forgotten came back. There had been a round of the girls all sharing their stories. Some were rather alarming, to be honest. Still, all of them were beautiful because it brought them to the places they were now with men that loved them without question. I'd needed a breather after that and made my excuses to escape to the bathroom, but Ember had followed me to share something she thought was important.

"I know you don't want to talk about Stone. I don't want to make you, but I need to share something. You've gotten bits and pieces about everyone's stories, and I saw that look you got on your face. They all had their man fight to have them. It's great. It's fucking awesome they had that, and I know why you're thinking you want that, too. But I had to be on the other side. Jager had a lot of demons. He still does. He wasn't going to fight for anything because he didn't really think it could or should be his. So I had to fight for both of us. And you know what? I don't regret one moment. It's easy to get caught up in hearing how their men all loved them enough to put up that fight, but I know I got to give that to my man. He loves me more for it because he'll never forget I made that first move. I'm not telling you what you should do, I just wanted you to hear there's more than one type of love story. It's just a matter of what you want."

She was right.

I'd walked away unsure, but right then, it clicked.

"Why did you call me bunny?"

Stone's fork froze on the way to his mouth, then he dropped his hand back to his plate.

"Finish your breakfast," he responded almost like I hadn't asked at all.

CHAPTER 15

Stone

SHE LOOKED SO FUCKING CRESTFALLEN that I couldn't contain myself. I pushed back from the table, getting to my feet.

Evie's eyes had dropped to her plate, an attempt to hide from me, to block out what just happened. I reached out to her hand, grabbing it in a firm grip to make my point. Her hand released her fork, then I was using my hold to pull her up.

"What—"

I didn't give her a chance to ask. I didn't have it in me to wait another fucking second.

I took her sweet lips.

My Evie melted, her body leaning into mine, her mouth following my lead as I tasted her. She was fucking perfection. The need that blazed through me at just feeling the softness of her lips move against mine almost brought me to my knees. My cock was throbbing, and even the pain of it felt good with Evie right there.

What felt even fucking better was the way she chased my lips with hers when I pulled back. The pull was too great, so I gave in. It was only when she pressed tighter against me, her hips stirring, that I pulled in all my restraint. Her body was asking for things I knew her mind wasn't ready for, and there was only so long I'd be able to resist the invitation.

The quiet, disappointed whine she made when I stopped made me feel like a god even as my balls ached at the sound. Soon, I wouldn't let her feel that need for even a minute. If she wanted me, she'd fucking have me because I'd always want her.

"Bunny," I called when her eyes stayed closed.

She caught my point, blinking up at me, waiting for more.

"I was trying to be good, to let you eat before we get into this. I promise you we're having it either way. Now, do you want to sit back down and finish your breakfast first?"

Without hesitation, she answered, "I'm not hungry."

She was, though. Maybe not for food, but the need was right there in her beautiful eyes.

"Come on," I said, taking her hand. "I'll clean this shit up later."

"Where are we going?" she asked, even as she came willingly.

"My room."

Her steps stuttered.

"Not for that. Not now." There'd be time. God willing, there'd be fucking decades of time. "We need to talk, and there's no telling who's going to show up around here."

"Okay."

By the time I got her back upstairs and sat her on the end of my bed, she looked near petrified. In that small space of time, she'd managed to convince herself this was going to end badly, and yet she hadn't pulled back. Her head was high like she was ready to fight me if I spewed more bullshit at her.

"I thought I should leave you alone, but Ember said she had to keep at Jager. She said sometimes you have to be willing to fight for what you want."

Yeah, Ember was fucking right. But it wasn't Evie who needed to do the fighting.

"I'm fucking crazy over you," I announced, not giving her any more time to stew in her worry.

Her lips, swollen a touch from me attacking them, gaped. Fuck, but I wanted to go right back there.

"You had me from that first time I came into the diner. No joke. It's why I ever came back at all. It's why I kept coming back, even when I told myself I shouldn't," I confessed. "I could spend hours standing here telling you every reason why, how fucking sweet and sexy and captivating you are. I could tell you every damn thing you said to me that sunk me that much more. I could tell you all the reasons until I was blue in the face, and I will if you ask for it.

"But what I need to say is that I fucked up. I fucked up from that first day. I fucked up when I didn't ask you out before I walked out that door. And I kept fucking up every day after that when I let myself decide what I thought was best for you."

The trepidation was gone in her bright brown eyes, and it let me take a breath before I went on.

"I've spent most of my life taking care of people. My mom was a good woman, but my dad was a deadbeat that took off on her. She never fully bounced back. I learned young to take care of her in what ways I could. When she got sick when I was sixteen, I was taking care of her completely. I did everything for her until I lost her."

"I'm so sorry," she whispered. Even when I was confessing to how I fucked us up all this time, my Evie still couldn't put a cap on her sweet.

Now, hoping that at the end of this, that sweet would be mine, I didn't contain my urge to kiss her again. I kept it soft and quick, but I took it all the same.

"It was a long time ago, sweetheart," I told her, speaking just a few inches from her lips, still holding her head in my hand. "I miss her, but it's not so hard anymore."

Evie, unable to accept that, leaned up and ran her nose along mine. Before she undid me, I told her, "Gotta give you all of this, baby."

She nodded, and even though it took clenching my hands to do it, I released her.

It took a second to get myself back on track before I continued. "In the Marines, I learned a different way, but it was still more of the same. They trained us to be ready to make the ultimate sacrifice for our brothers in arms, for our country, for millions of people here at home we didn't even know. I'd have done it. If the situation had ever called on me to make that choice while I was enlisted, I'd have done it without question. That training, that doesn't leave.

"Then I got out, and I had nothing to take care of. I'd fucked up my knee during a deployment. I wasn't much use to the Marines in the shape I was in, and the kind of work I could do didn't suit me. Even the military has desk jobs and shit, but I'm not that man. I left, and I was drifting. It was just getting through the days until I got a job in a garage that introduced me to the Savage Disciples."

Evie was hanging on every word. There wasn't a hint of doubt or distrust. What I was saying needed to be said, and yet I knew she didn't need to hear it. She was willing to forgive me without any of it. There was no question in my mind that I didn't deserve her, but that didn't matter anymore. Not as long as she would have me.

"The club gave me a new family. I think you're already seeing that that's what we are." She nodded firmly. "I needed that, and I thrived on it. They voted me in as president because I gave everything I could to the club from the day I was a recruit. I never asked for the position. They gave it to me.

"I told you about why I went away. When Daz ended up in that situation, I didn't think twice. I did what I'd been taught to do my whole life, I took the blow so he wouldn't have to. So Avery, Kate, and Owen wouldn't have to. It fucking sucked, but I don't regret it because that's what I do.

"But all that shit made me make the wrong move with you. I saw you, and I wanted something just for me for the first time since I got a fuckin' motorcycle after I was discharged. I wanted everything you promised to be, and everything that you proved you were in half an hour while I sat in that diner. Except you were so young. You were bright and innocent in a way that only highlighted that age difference between us. All I could think of was how it'd be for you to be on the back of my bike, how people would look at you and think all kinds of bullshit about why you'd be with a man like me, and it triggered that same response. Even as time went on and I knew you'd welcome me making a move, I told myself it was better for you if I didn't."

"And then I did it instead," she supplied, understanding in her eyes.

"Yeah, you did. And everything in me wanted to say yes, but I couldn't do it. I couldn't go against what I thought was best for you. Then I got locked up, and it only proved how right I was. I wasn't just some biker that was too old for you, I also had a fucking record. So when you gave me that sweet fuckin' kiss, I was even more sure that I was doing the right thing. But I was wrong."

Her eyes got wide at that, hope shining so bright it was blinding.

"I was so fucking wrong, Evie. You told me last night that you were going to fight for me, and I realized how fucking wrong I had it. Those people that'd think shit, they don't matter. None of that shit does, not if we don't want it to. The fact that I'm older, I can't change that. Fuck, I wish I could. It worries me to think about what happens if this lasts the way I think it will, and I end up leaving you long before your time. But my mom left this earth before she was my age. No day is promised. Getting caught up on that is only going to guarantee however many I have are a fuck of a lot less beautiful than they could be if they had you in them.

"I want you, baby. I want you on the back of my bike and in my bed. I want your smile, your laugh, those sweet fuckin' lips. I want everything you're willing to give me because I'd be a fucking fool not to take it all."

She didn't hesitate to give me even more. She was on her feet before I finished, her arms going around my neck as soon as I was done. Then she kissed me, and I knew it was her giving me everything. Just like I told her I would, I fucking took it all.

It was like holding back a rabid pit bull to keep from going after her mouth when she pulled back, but I managed it. Anything for her.

Her gaze cut through me like a knife. There was so much heat there just from that kiss. I almost missed her words because I was so busy staring in satisfaction at that look.

"But why did you call me bunny?"

Fuck, she never stopped surprising me. I started laughing despite the fact that my cock was trying to break through my jeans.

Reaching up, I tapped her nose with a single finger.

"You're adorable, most of all when your nose twitches. Like a bunny."

One of her hands left my shoulders and her fingers covered that nose. "My nose twitches?"

"You didn't know?"

She shook her head, still covering half her face.

"Whenever you concentrate or those couple times you got mad at me, you scrunch your face a little and it twitches."

She still didn't move that hand, but her eyes widened like she was freaked. No way I was going to let her think it was a bad thing. I swatted her hand out of the way and kissed the tip of her nose.

"I told you, it's fucking adorable. You stop doing it, I'll be pissed," I warned.

"Okay," she agreed, a small smile on her shiny, wet lips.

"Now kiss your man again, bunny."

She obliged, and it was fucking perfection.

CHAPTER 16
Evie

IT WAS OVERWHELMING, the feeling of having his lips on mine. I'd wondered so many times what it would be like, and experiencing it, I found I couldn't process the reality. It was all a blur of sensation. The pressure of his lips melding mine, his beard tickling my skin, his tongue tangling with my own. Then, there was the heat. So much of it, everywhere. My body was an inferno, but I never wanted to stop burning.

I moaned, unable to hold it back. Stone's kiss only intensified at the muffled sound, so I did it again. Before I knew it, I was on my back on the bed, his weight pressing me into the mattress. He felt good there, right, like I had always been missing him.

My hands roamed over every inch I could reach, feeling the hard mass of him. He was so powerfully built, and yet so gentle even as he kissed me deeply. It made me wonder what he would be like if we took things further. Would that power take over, or would he be careful? Or maybe he would somehow create the same incredible balance he did right then.

Just thinking of it turned my desire into a full ache. My hips churned, seeking some relief from the consuming need. Stone was right there, taking his weight off of one arm to clasp my thigh and firmly yank it wider. His own descended into the space he'd made, pressing right against me. I cried out, ripping my mouth from his without meaning to.

"Fuck, Evie," he groaned, his head descending to my neck. "You feel fucking incredible under me. Better than I imagined, and I imagined it was seriously damn good."

I wanted to tell him what that meant, to let him know how my heart soared hearing it, but it was as if my body had taken over. That relentless pursuit of relief was all I could manage. I rolled my hips, working my core against his hard thigh.

Stone's hand moved up my side, my shirt bunching and lifting away in the path of his firm grip. The rough texture of his hands somehow only intensified the sensation as he slowed beneath my chest. It wasn't even a conscious thought to shift in an encouraging way.

"Bunny, we need to talk," he said in a rough voice, even as he peppered kisses along my neck that tickled.

"No. Just more."

"Baby," he tried again.

"Honey," I replied, coaxingly.

He groaned but didn't give in. "I don't want to ask— fuck, I don't—but I gotta know what you've done before."

I knew why he needed that, and I knew I had to give it to him. I just hoped my answer wouldn't be like a bucket of cold water thrown over us both. Just the thought of how he might react had my throat tightening in that all-too-familiar way.

"I...I haven't...I've never..."

Stone's response was a long, low groan that shot right through me.

"Fuck. Fuck, baby. Fuck, it shouldn't matter. It shouldn't make my cock ache to think that no man's ever had you like this, but it does."

It was nothing like I expected because it was so much better than I could have hoped.

"Really?" I breathed.

Stone didn't answer with words. He shifted his thigh from between mine, I was choking out a protest when he pressed his hips into that space. The sensation overtook me first, but my mind cleared enough to see the point he was trying to illustrate. Or, more to the point, I *felt* it.

He was hard. Even through his jeans and my fabric shorts, I could feel the length of him. And when he rocked against me, I felt it slide against my sex in a way that stole my breath.

"Please," I moaned.

To my dismay, his hips backed away. I tried to bring my legs up to wrap around him, but it wasn't enough.

"I need to know what you're ready for," Stone said, his

voice even though I got the impression he had to put effort into making it that way.

"Anything," I answered by rote.

"No, baby. Don't give me the answer your body wants. You haven't yet, so I need to know what you're actually comfortable with. I won't have you waking up tomorrow and regretting this."

"I won't."

"Evie…"

Realizing how serious he was about this, I forced myself to focus on him. Even that only ratcheted up my need. His strong face etched into that mask of concern, his gray eyes awash with it. He'd lifted off of me farther, the cold air replacing his warmth against my heated skin. I lifted up onto a bent arm, too, following him. My free hand came up to cup his cheek.

"There was a time when I was saving myself. I did it because I was taught that it was what was right. But that was a long time ago, long before I even really understood what sex was because I wasn't taught that. I was just told to be a good girl and not do it. Then, I learned the hard way that a lot of the things I was brought up to believe weren't true. I figured out how to think for myself, and what I thought was that so much of it was wrong. I have faith in this. I have faith in you." His head dropped like it pained him to hear that. "I do. This doesn't feel new. This feels like something you and I have been on the road to for a long time. I trust you, and the only thing I know about sex is that I've wanted to take that step with someone I could trust. It's the only thing that's held me back since I left home. Now, I have that with you, so I'm ready."

He leaned in, kissing me softly before pulling away again. "Okay, baby. I hear you. Now, I need you to hear me. I want this, more than fucking anything, but I want to work up to it. Yeah? I want you to have time to enjoy all the build-up you should have, and I want to be in a place where I understand all you just laid out there before we go there."

"But…" I bit my lip, holding back the words I wanted to say.

"And we sure as fuck aren't going there if you can't talk to me," Stone added pointedly.

Oh, well. There was nothing for it. "It's just…don't you…need it?"

Stone gave a single bark of laughter. "Bunny, I'm pretty fucking sure I'm dying not being able to take you right now." I opened my mouth to argue against waiting then, but he gave me a look that made me shut it again. "I haven't had a woman in over two years. I can wait a little longer, knowing what I'll get is better than anything I've ever had."

There went my mouth opening again, but this time to gape at him.

"I…you…you haven't had sex in over two years?"

He grinned, and I was starting to think he found my

stuttering amusing. "I was inside the last eighteen months. Wasn't exactly getting conjugal visits."

"But, before that…or…"

"Or since?" he guessed. I nodded. "Before, I was busy. I'm not gonna lie to you. I've had a lot of women. You spend time around the club, you'll notice that part of the crowd that hangs around is women who are looking for that kind of thing. Used to be, I got a taste, I'd take care of that. But that shit gets old. I found I got the taste less and less. Except the fucking hunger I got being around you. And you came back into my life the same day I got out. Not just anything can satisfy that craving, so I've never tried to slake it with something else."

Wow. I didn't know what to do with that besides feel the immense sense of relief at those faceless women I'd been picturing him with over the last weeks disappearing from my mind.

"Now," he went on, "you going to give me a taste to show me just how right I was that you'd be sweeter than all the rest?"

With just that, the need came crashing over me again, pulling me into its depths.

"Yes."

Stone eased me back down, following me. His lips were a hair's breadth away from mine when he whispered, "Good."

This time, gentle wasn't the word that came to mind. Instead, it was like he was truly consuming me. He was hungry, and it was right there in his kiss and the way his hand retraced its path up my side without stopping. He cupped my breast as his mouth descended. First, down my neck, then dipping below my bunched shirt to wrap his lips around my nipple and sucking.

The pull and the wet warmth of his mouth shot right down between my legs. Like he knew how much I needed it, one of his hands moved down to cup me there. His palm landed right where I needed it, pressing right over my clit.

"Stone!"

He responded by rubbing in circles as he grazed his teeth over my trapped nipple.

"Honey," I whined.

He tore his mouth away from me and groaned into the valley between my breasts. "Fuck, baby. I can feel the heat of you through these fuckin' shorts."

I might have been embarrassed if I wasn't losing my mind.

"Don't stop," I pleaded.

"Not a fucking chance."

In a move worthy of awards, he slid his hand into my shorts, sliding through the wetness he'd created. His fingers went right to my clit, circling fast and pressing hard.

"Oh. Oh. Oh," I chanted, losing the ability to form full words.

"So wet. Shit. You're so wet for me."

He really needed to stop talking. I couldn't handle his rough voice saying such dirty things to me.

"Don't want to stop, but I need these fucking things off you," he said, tugging on my shorts to make a point. "I want my mouth on that sweet pussy. I want to make you fucking scream for me while I tongue your cunt."

Did I say he needed to stop? He absolutely did not. I was pretty sure just his words could get me there.

Though, when he got my shorts off and shouldered his way between my thighs, I forgot all about words. His words were only the beginning of the magic he could work with his mouth. Every flick of his tongue was better than anything I'd ever given myself. The pleasure was mounting and building toward something I wasn't sure I could even handle.

"Honey," I called again, feeling an edge of panic at being right at that edge.

Stone didn't stop. He pushed me right over when his tongue moved lower and pressed inside. I shattered in a haze of sensation and blinding light. My hips brokenly shifted against his face as my hands gripped his hair tightly to anchor me.

By the time any concept of what was happening came back, Stone was beside me again, his arms holding me close.

"Good?" he asked, a smug tone to his voice.

I should have called him out on getting a big ego, but he'd earned it. Instead, I just nodded. He kissed the top of my head and held me while the aftermath passed.

For the rest of the afternoon, we stayed right there in

bed. We talked and dozed. We even ate there after he ran downstairs to make us a couple sandwiches. He made me come again—with his fingers this time. And hours later, when I fell asleep in his bed with him, I decided that maybe alcohol wasn't so bad.

CHAPTER 17
Stone

EVIE WAS SPRAWLED across me when I woke to the sound of her alarm. Her soft tits were pillowed against my side, a smooth thigh flung across mine, warm against my balls. My cock was hard as a rock, and I wrapped my fist around it hoping to take some of the edge off.

The alarm tone stopped, then started up again before I felt my bunny stir. When she did, she blinked up at me and I found there was another time that nose twitched.

I had to tighten my grip when my dick decided to twitch in response.

Fuck, that was going to get rough for me.

She must have felt the movement because the smile forming on her sweet, drowsy face froze, and she looked down. Her body tightened against mine as she gasped.

Too fast. Fuck. I needed to get my ass under control before I scared her.

"Were you...masturbating?"

Her eyes didn't come back to me, and it made my dick twitch again. He was getting all kinds of ideas being the center of her attention.

I cleared my throat. "No. Just trying to take the edge off."

"Oh."

Was that disappointment?

"Oh?" I pressed her.

"I...um...well..."

It was. She was disappointed I wasn't yanking one out. My dick was fucking throbbing, more than happy to put on a show.

"You want to watch, bunny?" As I asked, I made a show of moving my fist up and down once.

Still not looking at me, she nodded against my chest. I'd let her make that play this time, but I'd be pushing her in the future. There was no room for shy when we were in bed—or anywhere else I might eventually have her.

I started jacking off, taking my time more than I usually would for her. My free hand roved up and down her curves, imagining feeling them while I was buried inside of her. I was caught up in my visions of her straddling my cock as I fucked up into her when her hand gripped around mine.

Jolting to a stop, my hand on her back shot to her chin to bring her head up.

"You want me to stop?"

She rolled her lips before finding it in her to give me the words even as her cheeks, and the top of her chest above those pert tits flushed a deep pink. "I wanted to help."

I had to bite down on my tongue to keep from blowing like some punk ass kid just at her saying that. Releasing my cock, I grabbed her hand. She came willingly, her eyes holding mine until I wrapped her fingers around me. I broke the connection first. Just the tentative touch from her soft hand had my eyes rolling back. When I looked down again, she was focused on my cock.

Closing my hand around hers and my dick, I showed her how. She tightened her grip with mine, pumped up and down like I led, but the feeling of it was all her. Evie was giving me that. Every throb of my balls, every tingle that gathered in the base of my spine. All of it was her. My girl. My bunny.

"Feels so fucking good, baby," I encouraged.

Her hand loosened and her fingers flicked out briefly. Taking the cue, I moved my hand away, and she immediately got back to it.

Her enthusiasm was what got me. She'd didn't go with my rhythm or pressure. She gave me more. Harder. Faster. She added little pulses of her hand that made me think of nothing but making her cunt spasm around me when she came.

It was too fucking good.

"Can't hold back," I warned.

She didn't let up, not even for a second. In a few more strokes, I was exploding. Cum rushed from my cock as I nearly blacked out. Evie kept at me until I was too sensitive to go on, and I flipped her to her back.

Not caring about the cum I knew was getting all over the fucking bed, I moved down her body and buried my face in her pussy.

Only when she went off for me, did I finally settle over her, press a kiss to her still-panting lips, and say, "Good morning."

I TURNED my bike into the parking lot, grinning.

Evie was working. Yesterday, she'd told me that she had applications for nursing jobs out since she was now finished with her program. Until one of those came through, though, she'd be working at the diner.

She'd made no bones about showing me how much she'd rather stay with me than come to work that morning, even curling back up in bed once she was already dressed. I was tempted to tell her to just quit. She didn't need to move out of the farmhouse any time soon—or ever, if I had it my way. She could coast until a hospital made an offer. The only thing that held the words back was knowing she wouldn't go for it, not even for a second.

Then, a different plan started forming.

I took a spot off to the side, away from easy view through the windows, but I saw as I approached the door that it didn't matter. The sound of the engine had given me away.

Stepping through the entrance, I met my girl's eyes from across the room. I didn't say a thing as she watched me walk toward her and take my old seat at the counter.

"Hi, honey," she greeted.

I'd never thought a woman calling me "honey" would do it for me. It seemed like something a suburban tight ass would have his wife call him. When Evie said it, it went right to my dick.

"Hey, bunny."

That smile she had widened, and it was enough to make me forget it was cloudy outside. For all I knew sitting right there, the sun was shining brightly.

"How's it going?" I asked.

"All right. It's been slow."

There were two guys in a booth at the other end of the joint. Clocked them from the windows before I made it in. One older than me, one in his twenties who'd been looking Evie's way.

Fuck, I needed to get my girl a property patch. Not that I thought she'd wear it much. Maybe to Disciples shit once in a while, but not to work here or once she was clocking in at a hospital. Hell, for all I knew, giving her one was setting me up to get a lot of shit about the "property" thing. Quinn, Ace's woman, didn't wear it. She was a librarian, sweet and shy as could be, but he'd shared how she'd gone full hell-on-wheels at the mention of wearing a patch. She'd chilled out about it once she undressed that it was a statement of protection more than ownership, but she still didn't wear it. From what I heard, she did keep hers safe, though.

Since I didn't have a patch to even offer Evie, I had to settle for the next best thing.

"You going to give me something I thought about a million fucking times sitting on this stool and give your man a kiss?"

Cue that fucking nose twitch.

Goddamn.

But even better than that was her rolling up onto her toes and leaning over the counter. I couldn't resist watching, seeing her gorgeous body bending, her expectant expression as she came close. I also couldn't resist knowing that fucker with his eyes on my woman probably saw it, too, so I let him get a good look before I wrapped a hand around her neck and got a quick taste of her.

The cook in the back called out that there was an order up, forcing me to let her go. She settled back on her feet, but those eyes stayed on me.

"Let me decide what I'm gonna eat." I let her off the hook.

"You're staying?" she asked, sounding excited.

I grinned. "I'll wait until you're done, then I thought we'd go out on the bike for a while."

It was good to see that the excitement didn't diminish, but ratcheted up a bit at that. She'd been anxious on the bike when I took her back to the farmhouse the first time, but that could have been about the state of things between us as much as being on a motorcycle for the first time. I wanted her to love being on the bike with me because fuck knows I liked having her there, even if I'd only had a taste.

"Okay." She didn't delay in going to get the plates for her one table, and I let myself think that hustle was about getting back to her man, not about doing a good job. These days, I was nothing if not optimistic.

While she hurried around the counter, I kept my eyes on her. I didn't need to look at the menu beyond the quick glance I got while she checked over the order. Nothing had changed. It'd been a while, but I still knew everything on it. This meant my attention was free to fix on her sweet ass as she walked, and then the guy in the booth, whose eyes came to me nervously before fixing on the table even when she set his plate down in front of him.

Since my girl didn't play games, and I wanted to give her the same, I didn't bother to move from having my back to the counter as she came back my way. I enjoyed the show in a way I knew she could tell since her cheeks got rosy by the time she was back and I was facing forward again.

"Did you decide what you want?" she asked, the pointed tone telling me she knew exactly what I'd been doing—both watching her and marking my territory. That flush told me that even if she gave me shit, she liked it.

"The cute waitress looks delicious."

The blush grew, and my cock responded in kind. "She's not on the menu," she sassed anyway.

"No," I confirmed. "She's not."

Evie rolled her eyes. "What do you want to eat?"

"Patty melt." She started to walk away to put my order in but stopped when I kept speaking, lower. "But I'll definitely be getting a taste of something sweeter later."

The way her eyes dilated, it was only the other people in this place that kept me from taking that taste right there at the counter.

For the next two hours, it was almost like shooting back through time. I was back in that seat, sweet Evie shooting the shit with me. She'd take care of customers when she had to, but always she'd return to that home base right across from me.

It was when she came back to me humming Simon and Garfunkel's "Sound of Silence" that I finally asked her about the fact that I'd only ever heard her singing things from before her time.

"I grew up in a very religious family. Father was a pastor," she explained. That right there raised as many questions as it answered. It explained how she was so innocent—in every definition—but it left me even more confused about what a sweet girl like her was doing on her own without any family supporting her and getting hooked to a man like me. "Our church was…more devout than most. You didn't just go on Sundays. Most of our parishioners were in three times a week or more. My father would do at least one service every day. One of the big things that brought everyone together there was a belief that most of society has strayed too far from the Lord's teachings. I was even homeschooled with more of the kids whose families were a part of the church because they didn't trust the influence of the school system."

Yeah, this was all making my understanding of Evie clearer and murkier at the same time. It was starting to sound like she was raised in some kind of whacked out cult.

"I know that face," she said, studying me. "There wasn't anything weird going on. Well, not really. It was just really strict, but in practice, it was no different than the typical church experience from what I've come to understand. No one thought they directly communed with God or spoke in tongues. There was no flagellation. It was very stringent, though. The word of the Bible was the highest law, and it was to be abided in all things.

"Anyway, that fear of corruption extended wide for my father. I wasn't allowed to watch movies that he had not approved first. We didn't own a TV at home, just the one at the church that had no cable. Then, there was music. He didn't allow current music at all. The only music I ever heard growing up was classical and religious hymns. He didn't even like the contemporary Christian artists because he said they were watering down The Message to make it more appealing to the masses when people should be coming to the church based solely on faith."

Yeah, so not a cult, then. It still sounded like a harsh upbringing for her.

"There was an older woman down the block, Mrs. Norton. She attended the church, but only on Sundays and holidays. To most people, she'd seem a very devout sort, but that made her sort of an outcast with the parish. Still, she was aging and living alone, so my parents both thought it was good that I started going around frequently to help her around the house. Mrs. Norton would go on to them about how much she relied on me, but I actually didn't do much. I think she just saw me being raised under my father's thumb and worried about me, so she kept having me over to socialize. She loved music, so she'd play all kinds of things, regardless of what my father would have to say about them. I used to worry it was wrong, but I never told him. That was where I learned it all. It was my first real experience in modern music, and I've heard plenty more since I left home, but those songs are still my favorite."

There was a hell of a lot there we were going to have to get into, especially that shit about how she left home, and why, but I felt like what she'd told me already brought me deeper into the heart of her than I ever had.

"It's good you had her. You spoken to her since you left?"

I watched Evie's face fall as the waitress coming in to replace her came in from the back and relieved her of duty. I didn't get an answer for a few minutes while she went back through the kitchen to get her things and clock out, but when she came back to me, she didn't avoid it.

"Mrs. Norton passed away about six months before I left home."

Fuck.

I pulled her into me, kissing her head. "I'm sorry, bunny."

"It was a long time ago." She tried to brush it off.

"Yeah, but that doesn't mean you aren't allowed to hurt," I told her. Her face turned up to me, and I saw the understanding burning in those eyes, knew she got how I still carried the burden of losing my mom. My bunny came up to ease that ache with a kiss.

"Come on," I urged, leading her out. "There's nothing better for that kind of shit in your head than getting out on the road."

And for the next few hours, with the wind, my bike, and Evie at my back, I was reminded how right those words were.

CHAPTER 18
Stone

"THIS IS FUCKED," Gauge muttered.

He wasn't wrong.

After arranging a sit down with Officer Andrews, I'd learned that shit with the Devils was worse than we thought. The Hoffman PD had already had a couple busts and four ODs that involved product branded with devil horns—their shitty, obvious calling card. The Devils weren't just making moves, they were moving the fuck in on our territory.

There was a time, back before any of the current members—besides Doc who came in when shit was coming to a head—that the Disciples weren't the club we had today. Drugs, guns, women, the club had dealings in all of it. The money had been good, and the thrill was too much a draw. Then, that shit nearly destroyed them. Brothers in prison, brothers getting shot. Even families were being targeted.

It wasn't an easy road for the small sect of brothers that wanted to see an end to that shit to get the club there, but they fought tooth and nail to drag the club out of that darkness and make it what it was today.

Since then, we've kept that shit out of Hoffman. We weren't the police, we weren't even fucking vigilantes trying to save everyone. People wanted to take the drive past the town line and get that shit, they did it and we didn't give a fuck. What mattered was that some assholes weren't going to be preying on our town, and we made sure anyone that thought to do so knew it.

The Devils would get one warning. No "three strikes, you're out" bullshit. I'd called a meet with their president to issue the statement. They'd either back the fuck off, or we'd do whatever necessary to make them.

Gauge, Roadrunner, Doc, and Tank were with me to deliver this message.

Which meant it was all of them, not just Gauge, getting pissed that we'd been waiting for going on a fucking hour.

"How the fuck long do we sit out here with our dicks in our hands while they pull this shit?" Gauge continued bitching.

Another time, I might have told him to stand down. Now, with the shit the Devils were pulling and the blatant disrespect they were showing by not being at the meet on time when us calling it meant they got to name the place, he was right to be ready to blow.

If they didn't show soon, the warning would go out the fucking window.

"Code is that we wait until that hour mark," Doc

chimed in. "We got fifteen minutes left. At that point, the fuckers reap what they sow."

There was no arguing that. It was the way shit was done. It was the way we worked. Gauge didn't have to like it. Fuck, I didn't have to like it and I wasn't while we stood in the fucking sun on a remote patch of land two hours out of Hoffman. It was just the way it was.

With just over five minutes left on the clock before we rolled out and started planning out a new way to deal with the bullshit the Devils were creating, the sound of bikes up the road reached us. My jaw ticked, and it was a battle not to reach for my 9mm watching those assholes ride up.

We'd agreed on officers for both clubs, which revealed a fuck of a lot when their president, Wrench, rode up with only one man at his back. The Disciples were a brotherhood. We voted in brothers that would help man the ship, a sign of respect for what they offered. Those asshole Devils weren't like that. Wrench had one man under him because the positions they had were about standing. Being the president was a power move for him, and he wasn't relinquishing that to a whole host of officers. If I had to guess, that VP of his would be out in a permanent way if Wrench felt he was a threat to that control.

I decided right then and there, if this shit really went to hell in a way I hoped it wouldn't, if we end up at war, I'd burn all their cuts myself. They didn't deserve to have that shit in the first place.

The two assholes dismounted and sauntered over like we hadn't been waiting. It was a power move, the same shit they probably pulled with their own club. Only difference was, it wasn't going to work here.

"Stone," the prick said.

"Wrench."

As I faced off with him, I could feel the tension from my brothers at my back.

"You called the meet," Wrench prompted.

"And you named the time. Maybe I'm feeling like makin' you wait."

The motherfucker grinned.

Fuck him.

"You got one week. I hear so much as a whisper that your asshole crew or any of that tainted shit you're peddling is in Hoffman after that, then we got issues."

Wrench fished out a cigarette, lit it, and took a drag before he even acknowledged that I spoke.

"Fuckin' A," he said, looking back at his VP. "The Savage Disciples think they still got some fuckin' pull in the world."

I wanted to wipe that smile right off his fucking face.

"The fuck you say?"

He took another drag, flicking his ashes my direction. "Your whole fuckin' club has gone soft," he spat. "All your boys getting pussy whipped, your ass locked up—not that you were much of a threat anyway. Your motherfuckers couldn't defend your turf if you tried, so we went for the opportunity."

The only pussy there was him, too fucking scared to declare war. He had no idea what actually fighting one was like.

Wrench started walking toward me. I saw what would happen before it did, what he was forcing my boys to do, but I let it.

Before he got within reach, I heard the click of a gun cocking behind me and knew it was aimed at Wrench.

"Another step and I'll blow your fucking head off," Gauge warned.

And there it was. This was meant to be a peaceful meet, and that shit was gone. Wrench might have been too much of a chicken shit to make the move, but he got what he wanted anyway.

Gauge had thrown down the gauntlet.

Wrench smiled again, and I hoped he had that fucking expression on his face when I put a bullet through his skull.

"See you around," he warned.

It was tempting, so fucking tempting to give Gauge the go ahead to take his shot as the two of them went back to their bikes, but it wouldn't change shit. If anything, it'd make all this even more fucked when their club retaliated.

This way, we had time to make our moves.

The two pricks were gone before Doc spoke, "You good, Pres?"

Not in the slightest.

I turned to face my brothers. "Patrols," I ordered. "Get a schedule together. And call all the brothers in. We got church tomorrow."

Without waiting to parse all that shit out, I went to my bike and got on.

Tonight, I'd go home to my woman.

Tomorrow, the Disciples would ready for war.

CHAPTER 19
Evie

I WAS in the kitchen at the farmhouse, trying to figure out what I might be able to make for dinner. Stone had left earlier, saying something about having to handle "club business"—whatever that meant.

For the first few hours, I had focused on applying for various nursing positions. Unless I had no choice, I wanted to stay in or around Hoffman. I had thought I might be willing to move wherever the right opportunity presented itself, but Stone and I were starting something that I had to believe would be worth staying for, and Stone had roots here. Besides, I liked Hoffman. It was why I settled in town in the first place.

I'd been volunteering at the hospital since I started my nursing program, and the rumors I'd heard were that at least two of the neonatal intensive care nurses were possibly moving away any time. If the whispers could be believed, that might mean there would be an opportunity to get the job I wanted right here in town.

If not, I'd figure out what I wanted to do when the time came.

While I stood there, staring unseeing at the pantry like the right combination of ingredients might magically come to life and dance around to give me some sort of direction, I heard the front door open.

Before the little feet running echoed in the hall, I figured it was Kate and Owen. One thing that could be said of all the bikers around was that you always knew when one of them arrived. You could hear those bikes coming up the drive every time.

I'd gotten to know both Kate and her son well over the last couple weeks. Owen was Daz's nephew. Kate had been married to Daz's brother until he passed away in an accident a couple years ago. She didn't talk about him. In fact, if the conversation came up, she usually tied herself in knots to avoid it. However, I could read how much she had loved him—*still* loved him. It was obvious in the way that air of mourning still hung around her, even if she lifted the shroud around her son.

"Evie!" Owen greeted with a shout as he ran into the kitchen.

"What's up, handsome?"

"I gotta pee!" Then, just as quick as he came in, he raced out.

I laughed, something I often did around Owen. I didn't know what Owen's father had been like, but he certainly took after his uncle. That little man was all personality.

Kate came in slower behind her son. When she did, I thought again that she really was a beautiful woman. She had perfect skin with a dusting of very light freckles that only made her more interesting looking. Those looks, though, only seemed to put her depression in harsher light. Every time I looked at her, I just found myself wondering how stunning she would be with a real, genuine smile on her face. I could imagine that her husband lived to see that. I hoped he'd gotten to see it often, and that someday, when she was ready, we all might get the chance to see it from her regularly.

"Hi, Evie," she greeted, even her tone was somehow flat.

"Hi," I greeted. "I was just figuring out dinner for me and Stone. Do you and Owen want to join us? I can make more of...whatever I end up making."

She gave me a smile that didn't reach her eyes, though it was still genuine. "Daz called Avery at the bakery. He wants to take us all out tonight, so we're good. Thank you."

Kate worked at Sugar's Dream, selling baked goods while Avery whipped them up in the back. I hadn't been over to check it out yet, but I needed to. Stone had been right about the baked goods being around regularly because of Avery, and as of yet, I hadn't had a single thing that wasn't absolutely delicious.

"That'll be fun," I said. I wasn't sure how going out with Daz and Owen could not be.

"Yeah," she agreed. "I think I'm going to lie down for a bit before that. Long shift. You know how it is."

I did, and I imagined they felt even longer for her. "Totally. Tell Owen he's free to come out here if he doesn't want to play in his room. I can keep an eye on him."

"Thanks, hun. I'm sure he'll love that," she responded before heading out.

I watched her go, struggling as I often did with the urge to try to fix her. It was the same instinct I'd always had that had led me to nursing. Unfortunately, I knew I didn't have the tools to repair what was hurting in her. I wasn't a therapist, and I certainly couldn't bring her husband back —though I wished I could for all of them.

Resigning to the reality of that always sucked, but I made myself do so and get back to the task at hand. Probably ten minutes later, I was pulling out everything to make roasted chicken and potatoes when that now familiar sound of motorcycle engines—if I was getting the hang of this like I thought I was, it was probably two of them— coming up the lane to the house.

Stone.

Just knowing he was back had a smile forming. It was probably a good indicator that I was in way over my head, but I wasn't going to focus on that. I was just going to ride the wave of happiness for as long as I could.

When Stone and Doc came through the kitchen, though, I realized that wave might be breaking on the harsh, hard shore sooner than I expected.

Stone's face was tight, his expression dark. Doc didn't

look quite so upset, more along the lines of tired than anything.

My throat tightened a bit with anxiety. I spoke through it anyway.

"Hey, Doc." He gave me a small, forced smile in return as I moved close to Stone. "Hi, honey."

Stone reached out and grabbed my neck to kiss my head like he often did with a murmured, "Bunny." That was good. The fact that he released me right away and walked past me wasn't. Stone was affectionate, I already knew in the short time we'd been together. He liked to demand a kiss or ask me about my day—or both. The quiet and distance were uncharacteristic and a bit alarming.

I looked to Doc in question, but he shook his head in a resigned way.

Unsure what to do, I watched as Stone got out a glass, then a bottle from the cabinet that housed all the liquor. I didn't get a good look at the bottle, but when he tipped his head back and drained the glass, I caught a glimpse of amber liquid disappearing fast.

Drinking didn't concern me. Stone was a grown man and a biker to boot. He hadn't shared that he was a recovering alcoholic, nor did he exhibit signs of being one currently. What was a tad worrisome was the way he immediately put his glass back down on the counter, filled and drained it again, then filled it a third time before walking out of the kitchen without a word.

I watched the place where he'd disappeared for a long moment before Doc cleared his throat and my eyes swung to him.

"That shit's not about you. Gotta know that, girl. That's just a man who had a long, frustrating as fuck day and needs to unwind," he explained.

That made me feel marginally better but still helpless. "What can I do?"

"Best advice I got is to just be there for him. Can't know if he'd want you close or if he needs that room. You gotta figure that out for yourself. Trust your gut there. Not my place to share any of what's eating him, and he might not feel he can either. Not to be rude, gorgeous, but that's just the way of it. Club shit sometimes can't come home. With him being the pres, any club shit there is, it involves him, so you need to be prepared for that."

I wasn't sure how to feel about that. It couldn't be said that I was thrilled about the idea of Stone keeping a lot from me, but that was at least in part because I was concerned about situations like the one we were apparently in the middle of, where he might need a way to get those things off his chest and not be able to. I could also understand it in a way. I wasn't a member of the club, even if I was involved with one. Perhaps some things involving the brothers simply weren't my business.

It would just take time with Stone to figure out if we could find a balance that worked.

"Okay."

Doc grinned then, and it was the real deal. "Gotta say, there was a time I'd have thought a sweet girl like you wasn't cut out for our world. Glad to see I was very wrong there. You got the chops to take that, process it, and come to whatever acceptance you just did, then you got it in you to stand by him in the way he'll need."

I didn't withhold my responding grin at his assessment. I wanted to be that, so I sincerely hoped he wasn't wrong.

"Gonna leave you to see to him in whatever way you see fit. But just to say," he looked around at the food I had out before focusing on me again, "you're cooking and feel like makin' some extra to fill an extra mouth, you know where to find me." With a wink, he headed out as well.

Trust your gut.

When he was gone, I didn't let myself overthink it. I followed his advice, which led me through the living room, and out the back deck where I could see Stone leaning against the railing and facing out into the yard. Without a word, I walked up behind him and hugged him. I laid my head against his back, right atop the Savage Disciples patch. The irony of that patch being between us wasn't lost on me.

Stone brought a hand to where both of mine were at his cut. I held my breath, afraid he was going to push me off, but he just rested his hand on both of mine.

"Not sure I can talk about this," he said after a few minutes of us standing just like that. "Not right now, anyway. Not when I haven't had a chance to bring the situation back to the brothers yet."

"Okay."

"I won't lie to you. Not ever. But there are things I won't be able to tell you. When that happens, I'll be honest about that, too."

Just like Doc said. "All right, honey."

"You gonna be able to hack that?"

"Are you going to talk to one of the brothers if there's something you can't share with me that's weighing on you?" I asked in return.

I heard him set his glass down on the wood railing, then he was pulling me by my wrist until I was in front of him, leaning my back to that edge.

"I'm laying that shit out about having to keep things from you, and you're worried about me?"

I cupped his cheek, his beard tickling my palm. "You've got a lot of burdens caring for the club. I just don't want them to overwhelm you."

He turned his head to kiss my hand, resting his lips there for several heartbeats before turning back to say, "I get to keep coming home to your sweetness, bunny, I'm pretty sure you won't ever have to worry about that shit."

I smiled then. I wasn't sure what I had done, but Doc was right. Going with my gut had definitely worked.

With any luck, he was right about it all, and I could be exactly the woman Stone, the man and the president, needed.

CHAPTER 20
Evie

"HOW'RE THINGS WITH STONE?"

That was the second thing Avery said to me when I walked into the kitchen after getting off work. The first had been a hello.

Since she was in there seemingly not cooking a thing, I knew what this was.

An ambush.

"Good," I told her, being mostly honest.

Something was up with Stone. It wasn't exactly a mystery. Since that night he'd come home from his business upset, the edginess hadn't left him. What was worse, I'd twice run into him talking to Doc or Daz in the house in hushed voices, the air of tension was palpable.

Something was up, but it didn't seem like it had touched Avery at all unless it was some unspoken rule that we weren't supposed to address it. From what I knew of her and the rest of the girls, though, I doubted that was it.

Whatever was happening, she—and likely all the women—were being shielded from it as well as their men could manage.

169

"Well, that sounds fucking boring," she muttered.

I actually laughed. "Should it not be good?"

"No," she backtracked right away. "I think I've just been desensitized to normal. I worked in strip clubs for years, surrounded by women who honestly—I shit you not —I think they created drama because they fed on it. It's the only explanation for some of the things that went on. Then, I got with Daz, who might be the biggest drama queen of all in his own manly-biker-way. But things have been so...quiet. The last bit of excitement before you showed was Ember finding out she was pregnant. Which was tempered by her freaking out about how Jager would take it. But even they fell into it pretty easy.

"I'm glad for you and Stone that this is happening and going well, but that doesn't stop me from being a nosy bitch and wanting a good scoop."

"Well, when you explain it like that, I feel the need to apologize," I teased.

She gave a dramatic, false sigh. "I'll survive. Especially if you spill the dirt about Stone."

"The dirt?"

"I'm not usually a keep-it-in-the-bedroom girl, but I've found myself very curious about what Stone would be like. Not like I want to try it out. I just can't get a read on him, and I've usually got a guy's number as soon as I get a good look at them."

I was pretty sure I was following, but I still found myself asking, "You mean...like sex?"

She smirked and said, "Yeah. You don't have to share if it makes you uncomfortable."

I appreciated that, but since there wasn't much to share, "We haven't had sex yet."

She blinked at me. "Really?"

The depth of her surprise made me bite my lip.

"Sorry, I don't mean to sound shocked. That's actually really great. Of course, Stone's a good guy so he'd definitely wait for you to feel comfortable with it."

Mulling that over, I turned away from her to drop my purse and keys to the kitchen counter.

"I think I'm ready."

There was no teasing or laughter at all in her tone when she responded, even though it was to my back, "You think?"

No. That wasn't right.

I turned back to her. "I know."

It was firm because it was the truth.

After over a week of being with Stone—that being, being with him in all ways without actually *being with him*— I knew it. I'd told him that first day that I wasn't fixated on waiting, but I'd undersold it. I was twenty-seven. It had only been over the last couple of years that I'd found the courage to experiment with pleasuring myself, but that didn't change the fact that I'd developed a sexual appetite. Since experiencing firsthand how much better Stone was at getting me there than I was, that hunger had grown ravenous. And being a woman of my age, a woman with a hot, talented man getting her off and sleeping beside her every night, that need was no longer satiated by his play. I wanted more, and I wanted it with Stone.

How she knew what I needed, how she understood that the statement was me fishing for advice, I didn't know. I just knew that she read all of that and gave it to me. "Then tell him."

It was just that simple and just that hard, wasn't it?

"I imagine you've already discussed this to some degree." It wasn't a question, but I nodded all the same. We had, more than once. We'd even had a conversation about birth control, which was surprisingly not that awkward for me when I allowed myself to step a bit into nurse mode. "So whatever experience you may or may not have." I felt myself flush as the indication that she also guessed I was a virgin. Was it that obvious? She went on, "He understands. What he can't understand unless you make it clear is where you're at right now. I'm not saying give him some impassioned speech or something ridiculous. I'm saying find a way to let him know. Honestly, there are a lot of ways that are just as effective with a man as any words would be."

She was right. How I would communicate it would take some thinking, but Avery hit it right on the head. Stone had made it clear that he wanted to wait for me. Now, he had to understand that there was nothing to wait for now.

If I wasn't up for communicating that, then I wasn't actually ready, was I?

"Thank you," I told Avery.

"Anytime." She grinned, no doubt reading that I was already half lost to her, making plans. It was time to send a message.

"FUCK, BUNNY," Stone groaned.

He was leaning back against the headboard, and I was straddling his thighs. It had felt like a bold move to climb on him like that after changing into the nightie I'd donned for us to go to bed, but it wasn't my doing.

No, I couldn't be held responsible for being forward at this point.

See, I'd hatched my plan to communicate what I wanted.

It wasn't a particularly complex plan, but I wasn't well versed in seduction. Step one was digging through the boxes I hadn't entirely unpacked in my room when I got home for the nightie I was wearing. It was sheer except at the breasts, barely made it past my hips, and was all around sexier than the plain cotton ones I usually slept in. I'd had it for over a year, buying it on clearance on a whim.

Until that night, I'd never even worn it. However, it was the sexiest thing I owned.

When I'd walked out of the bathroom, it was obvious in an instant that Stone agreed.

He'd looked at me for a long moment before he'd actually growled, "Get over here."

Thus, phase two of my plan had commenced. This being the part of the plan where specifics dried up. All I knew was that I needed to get Stone worked up enough to stop treating me like an innocent virgin—even if I was one.

Hence, the bold, jumping-on-his-lap move.

I was pretty sure it was working, what with his latest comment and the fact that his hands came right up to cup my behind.

No. Jeez, that sounded exactly like the sweet, virginal girl I was trying not to be.

My *ass*.

He used his grip to tip me forward, and I let him lean me into his chest. Knowing what he wanted, I jumped in to kiss him first. Already, I could feel the hard length of him beneath me, and I circled my hips against him as I teased his tongue with mine.

His fingers dug in, and I reveled in the feeling. I might have been making things up as I went, but his reactions led me to believe I was succeeding.

I kissed him long and deep, then pulled back to nip at his lips before going in again. His hands started to roam over my body, the thin fabric somehow making his touch even more potent. Which only made it more noticeable when his hands suddenly stopped on my ribs.

The change was so abrupt that it drew my attention from kissing him and made me lean back. His gaze dropped to his left hand at my side, then I felt it move.

I also felt the distinct scratch of the tag as he grabbed it from beneath my arm.

Damn.

Tags left on clothes? Definitely not sexy.

Before I could figure out how to get him to ignore it and get us back on track, his hold tightened, and he ripped it off. His eyes tracked the tag before coming to me.

"So, this thing is just for me?"

He sounded...pleased.

"Yes."

At my response, he gave me a salacious grin that I felt like an actual touch between my legs.

Okay, so he absolutely liked the nightie.

Since bold seemed to be working, I decided to put it all out there, even if it scared the bejeezus out of me.

"I wanted tonight to be special," I whispered, resisting the urge to blow out a relieved breath that I hadn't stumbled on the words.

"Why, baby?" he asked, his eyes and hands moving all over me.

Here goes nothing.

"I want you to make love to me."

Again, his hands halted. This time, I felt his whole body tense, too.

Not great.

"Bunny—" he started, but the words blurted out.

"I know you're trying to go slow and take care of me. I appreciate that, but I'm ready. I'm ready to take that step in general, but, more importantly, I'm ready to take it with you."

Those gray eyes stayed fixed on mine like he was searching for some tell that it was all false bravado. Although there was an undercurrent of nerves pulsing through me, I knew he wouldn't see any doubt because it wasn't there. I was ready for this. My only fear was that he'd turn me down right here.

Bold had been working, so I threw in one more move for him. Shimmying back on his lap, I brought my hands to the hem of the nightie and swiftly pulled it up and off. It wasn't like I hadn't been naked in front of him before, but he had always been the one to undress me until then.

When his eyes didn't leave my face, I felt the fissure of fear shaking my confidence. I'd expected more. I'd expected something from him other than…

The thought was gone from my mind when he flipped me onto my back, pinning me there with his legs still between mine. His eyes were dark, his face ravenous, and it made heat explode through me.

"Tell me you're sure, Evie. Tell me you're certain you're ready for me to have you."

Even as he made his demands, he was thrusting against me, pleasuring us both through his boxers and my panties. It wasn't near enough.

"Please, honey," I mewed.

He didn't let up that torturous roll of his hips, but he took it no further. "Not good enough, bunny. I need the words."

And with that, he gave me one final card to play.

Avery had said there were a lot of ways to communicate that were as good as words, but that didn't mean words weren't powerful.

Without any hesitation, not an ounce of anxiety holding me back, I decided to give him the clearest message I could.

"Fuck me, Stone."

CHAPTER 21

Stone

THE WORDS WENT RIGHT to my balls. They were barely dirty by the standard of other women I'd had, but from sweet Evie who I'd never heard even swear, they were fucking filthy.

They were also a demand I couldn't deny.

Leaning down, I pulled one of her pert, pink nipples into my mouth at the same time I cupped her pussy. She was so hot and wet even through the fabric that still covered her there. The damp spot forming made me want to thump on my chest like a fucking animal. Without even playing with her, she was needing me.

The urge to haul off and take her was overwhelming, but I couldn't.

Soon enough, I'd know the beauty of sinking inside of her, but getting her ready was my priority.

I rubbed circles against her clit, knowing the tease of having her panties in the way would only work her up further. My Evie was greedy. She didn't like to be teased; she didn't like to build up slowly. Playing around and not giving her what she wanted made her fucking wild. Each time we were alone, she reached that place sooner, the primal reaction stronger.

It was spectacular.

With tongue and teeth, I tweaked her nipples, moving back and forth between them. Not being able to focus on the pleasure in one spot had her trying to hold my head down, but she wasn't strong enough.

"Stone," she whined, already frustrated.

I dipped my fingers lower, lining one up on that damp spot, and thrusting in against the material. The tip just pushed between her folds but didn't fill her. When she started pressing up against my hand, lifting off the bed like she might be able to get me in deeper, I knew it was working.

That was when she started clawing at my shoulders, at the shirt I had on. Willing to give her that, I released her soft tit and sat up to pull it off. I should have known my clever girl had her own agenda, but she was too fucking distracting.

While I was still off guard with my shirt covering my face, she gripped the band of my boxers and yanked them down. My cock—rock fucking hard since she walked in in that nightie, and a hell of a lot worse after she asked me to fuck her—sprung free. It bobbed once, the rush of being free of the restraint shocking through me, but paling in comparison to the sweet agony of Evie taking me in her hands.

My little minx was trying to turn the game around on me.

With her pumping my aching cock, it was so fucking tempting to let her. I enjoyed it for a few strokes, my head dropping back. She'd learned quickly how to handle me just right, and her hands were so fucking soft as they ran up and down my length.

Her "mmm" as she played didn't hurt, either.

It was dropping my head to look down at her, her smooth skin and sexy fucking curves with just those little pink panties covering her, that got me back on track.

"Take those off," I ordered.

Her eyes flashed, and she released me in an instant to do as I said. Her excitement made her movements jerky, but it was better than any practiced show could have been as she brought her knees up to her chest to work around me. She wanted it that much. She wanted *me* that much.

I was one seriously lucky bastard.

When she got them out of the way, she settled back against the pillows, not even hesitating to spread her legs wide around me. For as long as I fucking lived, I'd remember that sight of her offering herself to me. I'd be on my fucking deathbed, and the highlight reel of my life would come back to that moment.

"Fuck, bunny. You're so fucking beautiful it damn near kills me."

It wasn't flowery. Not even close. There was a time I thought she should be with some fucker who would give her that, but I knew better now. That weasely asshole might have the words, but no man would feel her—all of her, not just that sweet pussy—lance right through him every time he looked at her. I did. I felt that shit in my heart, my gut, right down to my balls.

While I was content to just look at her, Evie wasn't so patient. She reached back out for me, but I stopped her before she reached her target. I grabbed both her wrists despite her gasped protest, and yanked until she was upright with me, wrapping her arms around my neck. Moving my hands down her body, I felt the outer curve of her breasts, the dip of her waist, and settling on the flare of her hips. With a firm grip, I hoisted her up and deposited her on my thighs.

I knew fuck all about how was best to do this, but my instinct was to give her some measure of control rather than just taking her. On my knees, with her straddling me, I edged us forward, knocking the pillows out of the way until her back was against the headboard. It took a single shift of my hips for my cock to settle right up against her hot cunt, and I groaned.

Evie rolled her hips, rubbing that wet on me and getting the pressure she needed against her clit. I kept one arm low, snaking it across her ass to help her move, and brought the other up to bring that mouth to mine.

She moaned into my kiss, working herself against my aching dick. She was drenched, and even not inside her, I could feel the way her pussy spasmed, wanting to be filled.

I didn't give in. Not yet. I took her mouth and let her work herself closer to the precipice.

I broke the connection to her lips only when her movements grew desperate.

"You're sure, Evie?" I rasped. The need I had for her was fucking all-consuming, but she still came first.

"Yes." It was a plea, a moan, a demand. All of them at once and no single word had ever sounded better.

Her thighs tightened against the outsides of mine when I lifted her up, a primal protest against stealing that chance to come from her. Her struggle ceased when I snaked a hand between us to lift and steady my cock. Unable to resist, I rubbed the head against her clit once, twice, but stopped before the third, after her broken, needy sound.

The kiss of that warm opening on the tip of my dick nearly made me black out. The feeling of it being engulfed in the tight hold of her cunt as she sank down on me made the world narrow until it was just us in that bed. The blinding bliss of her sheathing my whole dick when she slammed down made me bellow in ecstasy.

Both my arms wrapped in a bruising hold around her, pinning her against my chest as I buried my face in her neck and peppered her skin with light kisses. My crazy, reckless girl. I'd wanted to give her control to keep her from that pain, and she'd just gone in full force.

My head was a fucking mess. Nothing had ever felt even a fraction as good as being buried inside my Evie, as knowing that she was truly mine in that moment. And yet, knowing that she was hurting destroyed me.

Wanting to get her mind off the discomfort that still held her tense, I soothed my hands along her back, and let everything I was feeling pour out.

"Never in my life have I been given such a gift," I said, moving my lips across her neck and ear, reveling in the shiver and how it tightened the already impossibly tight grip of her around my cock. "This right here, right now, is the most incredible thing I have ever experienced. And not just the feeling of being inside you. It's *you*, Evie. It's you sharing something with me that you've never given anyone else. It's that you are more perfect than any woman I might have ever tried to dream up, and you're somehow here with me. It's the fact that every time I see you smile, a little more of my heart chips off into your hand. But in this moment, I'm not sure there are any bits remaining for me to give you."

As I spoke, her body relaxed into my hold. Then, her hands behind my neck started to rove my back and shoulders, sending chills rushing through me that made my cock jump.

"Oh," she cried on a breath the third time it happened.

A heartbeat passed before she lifted a bit, testing. I bit down on the inside of my cheek to keep from fucking exploding at the feeling of her moving that tight pussy on me. The groan of bliss and torture got caught in my throat as she pushed back down. She did it again, longer strokes this time before circling her hips and rubbing her clit against me with a gasp.

"Feel good, bunny?" My voice was like gravel.

She didn't answer, not with words. She lifted up until only the head of me was still inside, then came back down in one fluid motion. Then again and again.

"Stone," she moaned as she rocked up and down, taking my cock in long, slow movements.

"Tell me what you need, baby."

She didn't wait, didn't mince words. "More."

And hell fucking yes, I could give her that.

Grabbing her hips, I took over lifting her on and off my cock, pushing and pulling her and driving us both higher and higher.

"More," she moaned again, and I started thrusting my hips up into that heaven.

Evie gripped onto my shoulders hard, her nails digging in. I didn't care. She could draw blood for all I gave a shit then because I could feel her sweet cunt tightening. I could hear her breaths coming faster and shallower. She was right there.

With the last bit of control I had, I brought a hand up to pull her mouth to mine. A handful of thrusts later when she came all around me, crying out, I swallowed those sounds that were only meant for me. Her sweet pussy clamping down on me pushed me over the edge, and I exploded. Wave after wave of undiluted pleasure took me until it was a fucking miracle I kept us upright.

It might have been hours before my head cleared enough to find I was leaning against Evie, pressing her into the hard headboard. Cradling her lax sated body against mine, I laid us down on the bed.

I held her close as our heart rates slowed. She had drained me dry and filled me up. The sheer magnitude of all she'd made me feel leaving me nearly mute, but I gave her the only words I had left.

"My Evie."

And even drifting off to sleep, she found it in her to give me a little more.

"My Stone."

CHAPTER 22
Stone

I WOKE with my cock hard and throbbing against the warmth around it. Morning wood was a familiar feeling, especially with Evie sleeping in my bed. That delicious heat was not.

Half asleep, I rocked my hips once to take it all in. The jolt of pleasure woke me more, and I started to process what was happening. Evie and I were spooning, and I'd somehow managed to burrow my cock between her thighs, right up against her bare pussy.

I'd sacrifice just about anything to wake up like that every day.

But that morning, after my bunny let me be the first man to have her—and the fucking last if I had my way—was better than any other could be.

Just remembering the way it felt to have her tight cunt surround him made my dick lurch.

Pulling her even tighter to my chest, I lowered my head to bury my face in her hair. She smelled like berries. All the fucking time, she smelled like sweet, ripe fruit and it made my mouth water. I couldn't help but think that the rest of her would smell of sex, of both of us from the night before.

When she'd drifted off, I'd gotten it together enough to get up and grab a damp towel to clean us both off. She didn't fully wake when I'd wiped away our combined release from her thighs, and I'd felt a smug satisfaction at the fact.

Now, she was stirring again, and that included shifting her hips around in a way that had me biting back a groan. I tightened my arms, unsure if it was an attempt to stop her, or a silent request to keep going.

Her quiet, "Morning, honey," was raspy, and there was no stopping the surge of my cock against her again. She gave a little, "Oh," and I could swear that heat turned up.

"Morning," I replied, bending in deeper to rub my face along her neck. She squirmed more, tickled by my beard. The motion cut off sharply with a press of her ass against my groin. That time, I didn't hold back the rough noise I made.

"You're…"

"Yeah, bunny," I confirmed. It was unfamiliar territory for us, but the position and lack of hindrance was. There would be times where I could enjoy that for all it was worth, right then wasn't one of them.

Evie didn't agree. She circled her hips, exploring and probably reveling in the fact that I responded to her like she was my own personal goddess—because she fucking well was. It was when I felt the damp of her arousal wetting me that I knew it was time to speak up.

"Baby," I groaned, "not this morning. I don't want you sore."

"I'm good," she insisted, keeping up that sensual rhythm like she'd been trained to break a man's will.

"Evie," I tried again, but there was no missing that it was feeble at best.

"I promise," she pressed. "Just be gentle."

Gentle. I could do gentle.

Releasing my hold on her middle, I reached down between her legs and found her clit. With two fingers, I massaged the hard bud while I matched the pace with my cock moving against her. She moaned unabashedly, throwing her head back so the full length of her slender neck was bared for me. Licking, sucking, biting, I devoured her there while I drove her higher. I felt her pulse quicken on my tongue, her wetness soaking my cock and fingers.

Only then, when I knew she was ready, did I pull my hips back and angle my cock to slide inside. With slow, even thrusts, I sunk into her, feeling her tighten around me each time. And even when she begged for more, I didn't take her harder or faster. I brought her to the edge and went over with her just the way she'd asked me to.

Gentle.

BY THE MIDDLE of the afternoon, I'd have given my left nut to be back in that bed with Evie.

Or maybe I'd just hunt down that motherfucker Wrench, castrate him, and offer one of his balls instead to whatever god I could make that deal with.

"What the fuck do you mean we got nothing?" I demanded.

We were in church again. A fucking week of patrols and we had not one thing to go on, so it was time to bring all the brothers back in. It should have been a good sign, except their product hadn't disappeared with them.

"They've gotta be using local foot soldiers to get their shit out," Ham said.

"Or they're going quiet hoping we'll get complacent," Tank argued.

Could be either one. Could be it was some fucked combination of both.

"Jager," I called. "You get anything?"

The frustration clear on his face said enough, but he answered anyway. "Nothing useful. Fuckers are on the grid enough to know we got ways of tracing shit. Best I can tell, they're sticking to the old-fashioned methods so I can't hack their shit."

The best he could tell was probably about as good as anyone could. How the fuck he hadn't been scooped up in college to end up doing all kinds of crazy computer shit in some high-security government building somewhere, I didn't know.

This shit with the Devils stunk to holy hell. No one had seen a damn thing, and yet their product was still showing up around town. After my inquiry, Andrews had taken it upon himself to give me a heads up whenever he got wind of activity related to those fuckers. Another death and a hospitalization had been added to the count. Whatever the Devils were distributing, it was straight fucking poison beyond what that shit usually was. The cops were fixing to send a sample in for testing to figure out what the hell was in it.

If they had the opportunity to do that, the Devils were going to end up too hot for us to make our move.

"I don't want to go on the offensive. Not unless we have to." That got mixed reviews from the expressions aimed my way. Some of the brothers no doubt wanted to charge in, guns blazing, and shut those fuckers down. But that kind of shit ended with men in the Disciples patch in hospital beds and prison cells—if not chilling in a cooler at the fucking morgue. If the time came that we had no other options, I'd ride into war without fucking flinching. Until then, I wasn't willing to risk my brothers—especially not when so many of them had families expecting them to come home at the end of the day.

"We stay vigilant," I went on. "Patrols don't stop and security steps up for everyone. I don't know that those fuckers would go after the women or kids, but I doubt I need to say that it isn't worth taking chances."

At that, Slick—who was usually pretty even-tempered —looked like he was going to fucking blow. The man had a wife and two babies at home, and word was they were fixing to try for another. I'd never question for a minute that he was loyal to the club, but he loved his family more than anything.

"I'll go around, change out locks everywhere," he volunteered right off. It wouldn't likely matter since he'd put in every lock and no one called another locksmith in the event of an issue when he was in the club, but not one of the guys who went home to a family looked ready to protest.

Jager came in on his heels with, "Do the same. It's been a while since the last upgrades for some of the systems. Make sure everyone's shit is tight." His definition of "a while" was a matter of months, but the man didn't take his security systems lightly.

"Are we telling the women?" Sketch asked, not looking entirely pleased with the idea.

I thought about going home to tell Evie she was in danger because of the club. I imagined how much worse it would be to do that if we had little ones to protect.

"Personal discretion," I answered. "I'm not about to tell you what to share with your wife." There were times, rarely, when this wasn't the case. Shit came up where it was patched members only. This wasn't one of those times.

"We going ahead with the party this weekend?" Roadrunner asked.

It wasn't to me; it was to the room at large.

Hook piped in. "We don't gotta do that. I'm glad to just don the patch and call it done."

"Might be good to have it," Doc put in. "Those fuckers think we're occupied, might shake them out, make them sloppy. We could call in a couple of the Mayhem brothers to keep an eye on shit. You know they hate that crew near as much as we do."

I'd been debating putting in that call for days. The Mayhem Bringers MC was a crew in Portland. Ancient history between the two clubs wasn't great, but we'd resolved that shit when the Disciples went through the clean-up. Now, the two clubs would—and did, when it was necessary—go to bat for one another.

The only thing that held me back was that the Mayhem brothers were quick to do exactly as their name implied. Worse, their VP's daughter had gotten involved with a Devils member years back. It was nothing concrete, just a couple dates. Then, that fucking cretin had tried to force himself on her. Luckily, she'd been packing since her daddy raised her to. The incident had still nearly brought war between the two. If the Devils hadn't scraped that asshole off, taking his patch rather than facing Mayhem retribution back when they didn't have a prayer of withstanding that blow, the war we were standing at the edge of would have happened already.

Them leaving the dick to defend himself held that at bay, but I knew one call and the Mayhem boys would be all too ready to throw down. It hadn't been a move I was ready to make. Unfortunately, it was getting to be unavoidable.

If we were going to war, Mayhem would hear word and ride either way. Might as well give them the forewarning.

I looked to my VP, who was tightest with members of that crew. "Make the call."

There was nothing left to say, so I released the brothers to see to this shit.

Security, allies, and war.

But first, a fucking party.

CHAPTER 23
Evie

"SERIOUSLY, how the fuck do these guys always go through so much mayonnaise? We're going to have to get someone out here to do heart screenings for the lot of them. This jar was full two days ago when I checked, and now there isn't enough for the potato salad."

I walked into the big, commercial-looking kitchen at the Disciples' clubhouse to hear Deni voicing that complaint. The room was probably better equipped than the diner—not that that was saying a whole lot. Though, apparently, they went through comparable amounts of mayonnaise.

"That would be Daz's bad," Avery piped in from across the room where she was doing something at a stand mixer. "There's been two in there for a while because he opened a new one after a half-assed attempt to see if there was one in there. I moved the full one back on the second shelf, trying to get them to use that jar first."

Deni ducked back into the refrigerator while Daz, who I noticed was not helping, replied, "How the fuck is you hiding the full jar my fault?"

I was going to wait for them to finish their conversation —or argument, whatever—but Cami noticed me coming in and called, "Hey, Evie!" which led to a chorus of the same from the women and men assembled.

I waved, feeling a little awkward. Stone had been called away by a man who introduced himself as Roadrunner. If I remembered correctly, that was Ember's dad. He'd offered to escort me to the kitchen, but I told them to go discuss whatever needed discussing.

We were there because someone called Hook, who I hadn't met yet, was going from being a "prospect" to a full member of the club. This, to the Disciples, meant it was time to party.

"Hi, guys," I greeted. "What can I do to help?"

"First, come here and meet everyone," Ember called from a table where she was cradling her baby.

Unable to resist the pull of that little bundle, I went right over. Ember was a little less dressed up, but the bright red t-shirt she had on fit like a glove and matched perfectly with the red bandana she had tied around her head a la Rosie the Riveter.

"Do you always look that good?" I blurted.

"Yes," Max called in response. She was closing up a cooler that was filled with bottles and ice while Ham waited to carry it for her. "She even looked good right after giving birth. It was fucking crazy."

Ember rolled her eyes before saying with a tilt of her head toward the men standing around right beside us,

"That's Slick, Gauge, and Jager." I looked at the men who I knew to be Deni, Cami, and Ember's men. Slick and Gauge both nodded with smiles at their names. Jager just gave a jerk of his chin. He was intimidating to say the least. Ember, seeming to not even notice the serious scary vibes he gave off just standing there, went on, "And this is Jamie."

She lifted her arms away from her chest, an offer I took her up on right away. I carefully took the pink-clad bundle of cute from her. Even from the corner of my eye, I saw Jager take a step forward when his daughter was transferred into my arms.

"Back off, you brute," Ember warned. "She's a freaking nurse. She's got it." That wasn't strictly true. At the moment, I was still a waitress. I wasn't about to correct her right then, though.

Since the thought that unfriendly Jager was less than pleased that someone he didn't really know was holding his baby terrified me, I decided to focus on the adorable pudgy face looking up at me with bright blue eyes.

"And another one bites the dust," Daz sang.

There were chuckles all around, and they weren't wrong. I loved babies. I'd always loved babies. It was why, when I'd spent all those nights imagining what it would be like to pursue nursing, it was never a question that the neonatal unit was where I wanted to be.

Ember, ignoring Daz beyond a grin, commented, "She likes you. She's usually fussy when other people hold her.

Even me sometimes," she muttered the last, side-eyeing Jager. "If you can get her to sleep, I'm going to kidnap you when he's not there to put her down."

"I'm actually a cuddler when I have the spare time," I told her.

"A what?" Gauge asked.

"A cuddler. In the neonatal intensive care unit, they have volunteers hold the babies that can be held, or just be close to and speak soothingly to the ones that can't. Research shows the connection is beneficial, so they have volunteers to give that to babies whose parents need a break to get some sleep, or those poor little ones who have been abandoned or orphaned."

Something tense filled the room, so I looked up from little Jamie's drooping eyelids to see Ember's attention on Gauge. I turned my head that way, too, and saw his expression was giving nothing away. He took a few steps toward me, putting a big, heavy hand on my shoulder before walking past. He paused briefly at Cami to kiss her, then left the room.

"What did I say?" I asked Ember quietly.

Cami, though I didn't think she could have heard me, explained. "Levi, our son, he isn't mine. Not by blood. He was an accident before Gauge and I got together. Levi's birth mom took off before they even left the hospital. Gauge was there for the birth, but he wasn't at the hospital when she ran off. Levi was never really alone, but it's a sore spot for him."

"I'm so sorry."

She smiled. "Babe, he was overwhelmed because you're the type of woman that would go comfort those babies that were alone. There's not one thing for you to be sorry for." As punctuation to her point, she got right back to work on whatever food she was prepping, not going after him.

Things settled again, pockets of conversation popping up as I stayed focused on rocking at the rhythm Jamie seemed to like. It was then Stone came in, strolling right to me even as people greeted him with his name and "Pres."

He came to me, a smile in his eyes even if it was only a tip of his lips. Stepping up to my side and putting a hand around my waist, he kissed my temple and looked down at my adorable burden.

"You look good holding a baby," he said. There was still light in his eyes, but no teasing. He meant that, and he meant it in all the ways I could take it.

My brain went into hyperdrive, imagining up a future where I held our little bundle while he held me. A future where our child had the unconditional love I knew both of us would give, and the love of a huge, supportive family in the form of the Disciples if everyone I knew thus far was any indication.

Just the thought of it all took my breath away.

Unfortunately, it also distracted me from my bouncing, and Jamie was not thrilled. The sweet baby that she was, she didn't scream out and make a fuss. She just whimpered a bit. Of course, perhaps she had learned that more volume wasn't necessary since her daddy was right there taking her in his prominently muscled arms the moment she did.

Ember gave me an apologetic look, but I just smiled. Jamie was a lucky girl to have that fierce love from a man that I guessed didn't give that easily. And Ember had that, too, something I knew for a fact meant the world to her even if he exasperated her at times.

With my arms free, Stone grabbed my hand. "Come on," he said, leading me out. "I want to introduce you to the rest of the club."

"Oh, but I was going to help out," I protested. Slick had gotten to work shaping burger patties next to his wife who was elbow deep in what looked to be a punch bowl sized vessel full of potato salad. Cami was chopping vegetables. Meanwhile, Avery was still more efficient than anyone prepping whatever she was making, while Daz tried to sneak around her and get his fingers in the mixer bowl. I heard her snap something low about him being a "fucking cretin" to which he responded by slapping her butt.

"You can meet the rest of the kids," Stone pointed out, and the crinkles around his eyes told me he knew he had me with that.

"Okay, let's go." I tried to sound put out, but I knew I didn't quite succeed.

I HAD Stone at my side, my chair angled into his so my legs were slung across his, and Ash's one-year-old daughter, Evangeline, asleep in my lap. A few hours had passed since we'd arrived, and already I felt like I'd been a part of these people's lives for years.

The brothers, whether out of respect to Stone or because most of them had women I'd spent the night with a few days ago who had good things to say, had welcomed me with open arms—at least, Jager and the honoree of the night, Hook, did so to the degree I thought they were capable of.

Over the last hour, a variety of other folks had started arriving. I'd been warned that it would get crazier as the evening went on and more of those "hang arounds" showed, but it was still a calm barbecue atmosphere at the moment.

At least, that was the vibe until a shaggy-looking blond man came around into the clubhouse yard. Almost as one, the brothers near me seemed to go on alert, and then the outright aggression was so startling I was shocked Evangeline didn't wake.

Stone muttered to no one in particular, "Get that motherfucker off our property."

Ham, Gauge, and Tank—Cami's dad—took off without hesitation. I tracked them as they made it across the yard and circled the man. He didn't look particularly keen to leave, which I thought—what with the way Ham stood there staring him down with arms crossed over his chest—was not a wise decision at all.

"Um..." I hesitated, not knowing if it was my business, but asked anyway, "what was that?"

There were a couple throats cleared before Stone answered me. "That guy, he was seeing one of the dancers at Candy Shop a while back when we first bought it." He paused for a long moment while I just watched him staring across the yard where the guy had been muscled away. "She came in with a black eye one night. She tried to deny it but eventually told Daz the asshole hit her. We sent a couple brothers to show him how we felt about that. He knew he was not welcome anywhere near the club again. Not ever. No motherfucker that would take his hands to a woman is."

Those words, the vehemence and underlying violence to them, shook me right to my core. Stone wasn't looking my way, but I stared at his hard profile, feeling my chin start to tremble, my throat getting tight.

"Evie, you okay?" I think it might have been Ash that asked, but I wasn't sure.

Her calling my name brought Stone's attention to me. "Bunny?"

"That's…it…it's good you believed her," I stuttered out.

"Of course we did. Would have even if she didn't have a bruise," he said, his face concerned.

"Not everyone would."

I felt his eyes on me, but my focus was all on Stone. He shifted forward in his chair, leaning toward me. "Sweetheart?"

"I was engaged," I blurted. Why? I didn't know. Once I'd said that, though, I had to keep going. Stone's face had shown a flash of surprise and then locked down. I didn't know what that meant, but I couldn't let him believe for a minute that there was someone else that meant what he did in my life because there hadn't been. "Well, I don't know. Maybe betrothed is a better word? He didn't propose to me as much as shake hands with my father and agree to get me and my father's job when he stepped down." Stone was the only one who understood what that job was, but I also wasn't telling anyone else this story. It was for him; I'd just put myself in the uncomfortable position of telling him when we had an audience. "I didn't know him well, and I didn't like him, but it was my place. So, we started dating, sort of. And he…he wanted…to take liberties." I felt ridiculous saying it that way around a bunch of bikers, but I couldn't quite break that ingrained mentality to not speak of such things. "When I refused, he backhanded me."

If I thought the feel had been electric before, I was grossly mistaken. The pure lightning that came from Stone now was otherworldly. His face was tense to the point his jaw ticked, and his eyes were blazing.

"It was just the once. I barely knew him, and I didn't like him. With that, I was done. I went to my parents to tell them I wouldn't marry him. They didn't agree."

I heard a muttered, "What the fuck?"

Stone didn't say a thing, but he looked ready to rip the world apart, such was his rage.

Then, there was a loud snap and my eyes flew to the shattered arm of the lawn chair that was held between his two hands.

"Honey," I whispered in shock.

But before either of us could say anything else, we heard a roar from inside the clubhouse and a yelled, "Call a fucking ambulance!"

CHAPTER 24
Stone

MY BLOOD WENT from boiling to solid ice at the sound of Jager's yelling.

I was on my feet in a second, running for the door with the others.

When I saw the brother inside, I froze.

Ember was sobbing, holding baby Jamie to her chest. Jager's hands were on the bald sides of his head, his fingers yanking on the undone line of hair that usually made up his Mohawk. Roadrunner was behind them, frantically yelling into the phone that his granddaughter wasn't breathing.

Wasn't. Breathing.

Everyone was horrorstruck by what they were seeing, until I felt myself shoved to the side.

Evie came barreling through, a woman on a fucking mission.

"What happened?" she demanded, no-nonsense and more in command than I'd ever seen her.

"She...she...she..." Ember tried to get out, struggling through her sobs. "She was eating and..."

Evie didn't wait for anything else. Without apology or finesse, she reached out and grabbed Jamie from Ember's arms. I saw Jager react and move on instinct to hold him back. I had no idea what to do, but I knew without question that my girl did.

Dropping to her knees with an unchecked thud, Evie turned the baby onto her stomach across her thighs and one arm. She used the heel of her hand to pump five times against Jamie's back. A small spray of spit up came out onto Evie's knees, but she didn't hesitate. With careful, but efficient movements, she turned the baby over onto her back on the floor. After checking her over, she started pressing with her fingers on Jamie's chest. Nothing happened.

Jager struggled against me, desperate to get to his little girl, but I held him back, Hook coming over to help me.

I watched, fucking terrified, as Evie started doing CPR. There was no hesitation, no fumbling at all as she cared for the tiny girl. After two rounds of breathing for her and chest compressions, Evie paused a little longer when she listened to her chest.

"She's breathing," she announced. Jager sagged against me until I was taking his full weight. Ember collapsed to the floor right where she was.

I heard Tank, who must have taken the phone from Roadrunner, filling in the 911 operator. "She's breathing. How far off is the ambulance?"

Jager regained his feet, moving over to fall to his knees beside his woman and Jamie.

"Don't move her," Evie instructed as he reached out to his daughter who was now coughing and moving her limbs. "It's best to get her checked out at the hospital first."

Jager, his face still pale, looked at her. I braced to jump in, unsure where the fuck his head was at, but I didn't need to. He shuffled forward a few inches and yanked my girl into his arms. I'd never seen him hold any woman besides Ember, but he wrapped Evie in tight.

"Thank you," he rasped brokenly.

She hugged him back for a moment, though her expression had been shell shocked at first because that was my girl. Even after giving us all the greatest gift she could offer, she willingly gave more when she knew the brother needed it.

And right then, I knew without a shadow of a doubt. Even if it was too soon, even if I'd never experienced it before, even if it seemed fucking crazy, I'd never been more sure of anything.

I fucking loved this woman.

The sound of the sirens came after a minute, but what might have been too late if it weren't for Evie.

As the paramedics rushed in and saw to Jamie with Evie explaining everything she could, I thanked every fucking force in the universe that I'd walked into that diner two years ago.

God fucking willing, I'd be saying those thanks for the rest of my days.

HOURS later we were pulling up to the farmhouse.

The party came to an abrupt end with Jamie's accident. After clearing out the yard, the actual Disciples family hunkered down for news about how the little one was. Roadrunner, Evie, and I went to the hospital where my girl went out of her way to speak to people she knew and get us updates.

We finally left when Jager came out, explaining that they wanted to keep her overnight as a precaution. Roadrunner, worried about his granddaughter and how the situation had impacted his own daughter, stuck around.

None of us had spoken much in that waiting room. Everything that had happened today weighing on us all. I'd thought about coming up with something to say as I'd walked Evie out to my bike, but nothing came out.

I'd learned a huge, unpleasant chunk of her history that I couldn't even think about without my blood pressure sky-rocketing, I'd watched her save the life of someone I loved, and I'd handed my fucking heart over to her—whether she knew that yet or not. All this after Roadrunner filling me in when we got there that the Devils had sent a couple of their lowlife thugs into our turf that night like we'd expected. It was time to act, and Mayhem was with us.

I'd never in my life been so drained and high strung at the same fucking time.

Even as I stopped the bike and let Evie get off, words escaped me. She was still climbing off with big steps. I hadn't had the heart to tell her she didn't need to do that, just avoid the pipes. It was too fucking cute to see her do it.

I came around and put a hand on her back to lead her inside, but she didn't move with me.

"Are you okay?" she asked instead.

Not exactly.

"Fine, babe."

"I…um…well…" It took her a minute to put the words out there. "I'm sorry for telling you about Isaac that way. With everyone there, I mean. I meant to just tell you, but hearing how you'd handled that other guy just…"

Just made her feel safe.

Reaching out, I cupped her smooth cheeks in my hands. Fuck, she felt so fragile. How any motherfucking cunt out there could lay a hand on her, floored me. I was afraid I'd hurt her just trying to handle her with care. Yet, she was so fucking resilient. She left that shit behind, abandoned everything she'd been raised with, built a life for herself, and managed to be the type of woman that acted and saved a life when most people would panic.

"I'm not mad at you, bunny."

"You're not?"

Shit. She really thought I would be?

"No. I'm fucking furious that some asshole put his hands on you. That doesn't happen, not with me around and not to my fucking woman. I snapped that chair because it was that or demand you tell me where to find him so I could snap his neck." Her eyes widened in horror, but I didn't take it back. She had to know the type of man I was, the man I would always be, if she was going to let me be a part of her life. "But I'm not mad at you. I don't care how you told me. I'm just glad you did, even if I fucking hated hearing that."

"Oh, okay."

"I'm sorry you thought I was," I said, leaning in to kiss her forehead. "There's just so much shit happening all at once. I got into my own head, but it wasn't me trying to hold back from you. Yeah?"

"Yeah."

When she looked up at me like that, pure hope in her eyes, looking like a goddamn angel, I wanted to tell her exactly what I felt. Instead, I went over different ground we needed to cover.

"What happened when you told your parents what that fucker did?"

She pulled back, but not to deny me that. I watched

her take a few steps into the dark yard, like she needed space to get her head together. I could grant her that…barely.

"They told me that if he was unhappy, I must not be fulfilling my duties to him well. I tried to tell them that he was pushing me sexually, thinking that would bring them around since they were vehemently against sex outside of marriage, but they didn't believe me. They just said that the fact that I would tell such a lie about him was precisely why I had earned what he did."

Not even imagining the sound of the cell door closing every day when I was inside lessened my desire to track that cunt down, and her fucking parents while I was at it, and teach a few lessons.

Evie kept on. "It was then I really let myself think about the way they had treated me. My whole life, I'd swept things under the rug. I blindly accepted it when they said I wouldn't go to college, but become a pastor's wife. I accepted the strict rules, the 'woman's place' lectures, the constant criticism and belittling. But right then, when he'd hit me and they tried to make me feel as if it were my fault, I knew that I wasn't the one that was wrong. They were. They always had been. So, I spent the next two days getting my things together when they were busy, and then I left."

"Just like that?" I asked, my voice grating against the desire to fucking let loose about those pricks.

"Well…no. I made my statement first," she evaded.

Coming up behind her, I wrapped my arms around her middle and said into her hair, "You wanna explain that?"

"I...um...I was in charge of making the pamphlets for each Sunday service at that point. They had all the names of folks who needed prayers, announcements, schedules for the week, stuff like that. I made them on Saturdays and put them in all the seats so everyone would have them Sunday morning.

"Isaac hit me on a Thursday. That Saturday, I went into the church office like I was expected to, and my father had left his notes about what to put in as usual. It even included the fact that Isaac would be giving part of the sermon the next day. I just...lost it. Instead of including anything I was supposed to, I made an entire flyer about what Isaac had done, and what my father said. I even got out the camera we had and took a picture of the bruise on my cheek to put in it. I printed it out and put one in each seat. That next morning, when my parents left for the service, I called a cab to take me to the bus station."

I couldn't help it, I started chuckling. I'd been thinking along the lines of going to the cops, not trying to reveal to all the church what a dick the fucker was.

"What?" she asked.

"Bunny, that shit sounds like it's out of some stupid teen movie. Some guy's a dick, and you made a damn flyer about it."

She sighed. "It was stupid. It probably didn't even matter, but I was so mad."

"I piss you off, you gonna put up posters in the clubhouse about it?" I teased.

She turned in my arms, swatting at me with a ridiculous pout on those puffy lips. "You watch yourself, mister, or I just might."

Christ, she was fucking cute.

I leaned down to kiss her. "I'll try my best, baby."

"See that you do."

"Though, might put up some posters myself. Something to show how fucking proud I am to have a woman that could do what you did today."

She melted into me. "It was nothing."

"You saved her life. Someone might have been able to get walked through that shit by the 911 operator, but you were already halfway to getting her breathing again before that could have happened. That's my niece—maybe not by blood, but that's just bullshit semantics. I don't think it was nothing, and I know Jager and Ember don't. No one that was there thinks what you did was nothing."

"He hugged me," she whispered in awe.

"Yeah, bunny. And I'm thinking you get how big that was. Jager isn't the type. A lot of the guys, they'll be affectionate with you in their own ways. You'll be part of the family. Jager would lay down his life for anyone in the club, including doing that for any brother's woman or family, but he doesn't do the rest. I've never seen him treat anyone but his woman or his daughter like that."

"Wow."

"Yeah, wow," I echoed. "You earned that from him. You earned the love the club's got to give from all of us with that shit."

Her eyes grew huge. "All of you?"

Oh, yeah, she caught what I was implying there.

"Yes, Evie. All of us."

Her eyes glistened in the moonlight as tears gathered at the edge. "Stone…"

"I love you, bunny."

She face-planted into my chest, wrapping her arms around my middle and squeezing for all she was worth.

"You take your time getting there. I'll wait however long you need, but you gotta know you have that from me."

Her head popped up, and I learned there was another time her nose twitched. One I would never forget in all my days.

It was right before she said, "I love you, too."

CHAPTER 25
Evie

STONE STARED AT ME, those gray eyes edged with disbelief like it wasn't possible that I'd really said those words.

Then they changed, but it was impossible for me to get a look at him because he dropped his lips to mine and kissed me. It was different than before, wilder, like some part of him had always been leashed, but me saying I loved him had broken that tether.

I was gasping for air by the time he pulled back, his face hard but his eyes bright. I knew that look, though it had a new edge now. He wanted me, right then. Instead of having to push him at all like I might normally, he reached low and grabbed me behind the thighs without a word, hoisting me up. By rote, I wrapped my legs around him, and we were moving.

I bit back a laugh at his quick, determined stride across the deck and through the back door. We made it through the living room and were passing the kitchen when we heard Daz.

"Way to go, Pres," he cheered.

Stone didn't so much as break his stride, and that laughter bubbled out of me. Even the desire heating within me at Stone's need couldn't overpower the pure joy I was feeling.

Stone loved me.

There was no way to count how many times I'd imagined him saying those words. It was a dream that had started back when he first started coming to the diner, and only gained momentum when he came back into my life. Experiencing it, actually being able to look into his gruff, handsome face while he gave me that, there was nothing on Earth that meant so much to me.

While he climbed the stairs at nearly a run, I realized I'd been wrong, sitting in my car weeks ago, believing God hated me. No, the fact that Stone came barreling into my life again right then showed me it was the exact opposite.

"Stone," I started, overwhelmed with the need to say it again.

"No," he bit out, startling me.

"What?"

"You wait. You don't say those words again until I have you in my bed. You don't say them until I can look in your eyes while I'm buried inside you when you give me that."

Did I say the joy was outweighing the desire?

I was wrong.

Very, very wrong.

"Okay," I squeaked.

"That's my good girl," he returned, already alighting at the top of the stairs.

Why did the words only excite me more?

We made it to his room, but he didn't take me to the bed as promised. He spun us, slamming the door, and then pressing me up against it. Before I could say a thing, his mouth was back on mine. I opened in an instant and his tongue dove inside. His kiss was aggressive, powerful and trying to return it felt like battling. We were fighting to show each other the depth of what we were feeling, and no war had ever been so sweet.

He had me pinned to the door by his hips between my legs, his torso against mine. His hands moved from my thighs, up under the skirt of my dress to cup my ass. They were so big I could feel the tips of his fingers just at the seams of my panties. I wanted so badly for him to move them closer together, to go beneath that fabric and fill me.

Shifting my weight in his hold, he started to move us away from the door. I clutched onto his shoulders hard with both hands, ripping my mouth away to say, "No."

He slammed me right back against the door, leading with his hips and rubbing against my clit in the best way.

"You want me to take you right here?" he demanded.

"Yes," I moaned, far past the point of caring how wanton it sounded.

"Fuck, I love you," he grunted.

I wasn't able to respond in kind, his order not to be damned when his hand dove in, giving me exactly what I wanted. There was no prelude, just two of his fingers driving inside, filling me up.

"Yes!" I cried out.

"So soaked," he muttered with approval.

I rocked my hips in the small measure of space I had, desperate for more.

"You want it, don't you? You can't even wait."

"Please," I begged, the only confirmation I could give.

His fingers left, but he wrapped them around the gusset of my panties. I wondered for an awestruck moment if he was going to rip them off, but he just held them to the side while he rubbed his cock against me until the head caught at my entrance.

"Eyes," he demanded.

I blinked them open, looking directly into his. Only then did he slam home.

He didn't hold back. He didn't wait a moment for me to move, to show I had adjusted to the size of him that still came with a tinge of pain each time. He just gave us both what we needed, slamming in hard and deep.

I dropped my head back against the door, eyes shutting, when he bit out again, "Eyes, Evie."

I forced my neck to straighten, my focus to fix on his eyes that looked like silver fire.

"You don't look away," he ordered. In that instant, he was every bit the president, even if everything but the two of us had ceased to exist.

"Yes, honey," I answered.

"You keep those fucking eyes on me until you come, and you do that with the words I want to hear on your lips. Yeah?"

His thrusts grew more powerful like he thought I might deny him.

"Yes."

"You say my name. My real name when you come."

I blinked in surprise. He'd shared his real name before he'd become Stone, but he told me that didn't feel like him anymore. I understood, having not been Genevieve since I left home. But to have him now, to share what we were, we both had to give it all.

"Yes."

Then, he gave it to me harder. A reward.

"Yes, baby," I moaned, wanting more.

He gave it to me. I kept repeating it, again and again as he drove into me more ferociously each time.

Right when it was too much, when I couldn't hold back the wave of pleasure that threatened to take me under, I gave him what he wanted.

"I love you, Austin."

And I erupted.

There was nothing but the cresting ecstasy moving over me, the primal way Stone stared at me as he followed me over, the animalistic sounds he made as he did.

There was no world, no me, no Stone. There was just us. Just this single moment of absolute bliss.

IT WAS a long time before either of us said anything.

Stone had moved us from the door, laying down on the bed with me on top of him, our connection unbroken.

We laid there a long time, coming down from the high before he spoke.

"Never thought I'd have this."

I was tempted to rise up on my arms to see him, but I sensed he needed to say this without interruption.

"Watched my brothers find it, and I can't deny I was jealous as fuck. Every night, I'd come back to this bed or crash at the clubhouse telling myself that I had the club. I had this whole family in them, and that was enough. But it wasn't. Not really.

"Then I met you, and I was so fucked over it. Thinking I shouldn't have you, thinking it was wrong. I never let myself get far enough past the wanting to realize that you might be it. Exactly what they'd found. Exactly what I'd wanted."

I felt tears stinging my eyes, but I stayed where I was until one of his big, warm hands cupped my cheek and pulled me to look at him.

"And now here you are. Like a fucking dream every minute. Making me the luckiest bastard around."

I chuckled even as one of those tears escaped. Then, in a watery voice, I said, "I love you."

"Lucky as fuck," he muttered again, "to have that from you. Any man would be. I can hardly believe it's me."

I crawled up him a bit, losing a breath when he slid out of me. When I had my lips right over his, I whispered, "It's you."

He kissed me, light and sweet. So at odds with what we'd just shared, and so absolutely perfect.

He broke it after a long moment to mutter, "Shits me, 'cause I don't want to move from this spot, but we made a mess we gotta go clean up."

I pinched my lips together. He wasn't wrong. I could feel the evidence of that on my thighs and spreading even as he said it. My face scrunched up at the feeling, and he smiled. I knew it was because my nose had twitched, something he liked to point out often.

"Yeah, we should do something about that."

He gave a light, playful swat to my behind. "Up, bunny. Gotta get my girl in the shower."

I was getting to my feet as he said the last, and I froze for a second. That was something we hadn't done yet. It wasn't like I was such a prude I didn't know it was done. It was simply new.

Stone caught the look of surprise and—I knew, even if I could see it—excitement on my face and grinned. He could be so cocky sometimes. "Yeah, baby. Figured you telling me you love me is worth two new experiences."

I flushed, glancing at the door, then the bathroom. That grin was still on his face when I looked back.

"I think you're right."

He didn't waste another second before he got up, led me into the bathroom, and introduced me to shower sex.

Which, incidentally, was amazing. Though, door sex would now probably always be my favorite.

CHAPTER 26

Stone

"VIC'S BREATHING DOWN MY FUCKIN' throat," Roadrunner muttered. "They want a strike. Full offensive. You know how they are."

Vic was one of the Mayhem boys that Roadrunner had been tight with for years. And, yeah, I knew how Mayhem was. I'd known it before I gave in and brought them into this fucked situation.

"Shit's coming to a head, one way or another," I said.

"You thinking of making that move?" he asked.

I had not one fucking clue what to do. That shit with Jamie and everything that happened with Evie later that night had me at sea on the whole thing. I didn't want to put myself or any of the brothers in danger, but the shit the Devils were pulling couldn't stand. It wasn't just about pride or saving face, even if the police went ahead getting their rancid shit tested, and they were eventually taken down, it wouldn't change that we hadn't put a stop to their shit. The Devils weren't the only organization that would want to get a foothold around here if they could. There was a message to be sent here.

"We're going to have to. No fuckin' choice with this shit they've been pulling. I'm just looking for the move that had everyone on our side walking out unscathed."

Roadrunner didn't respond. That was the big question. How?

We both sat outside the clubhouse, eyes on the forecourt, not having an answer.

"Want to get Jager on a recon. Know he didn't find anything first go, but we gotta know where they're at. The quantities of shit they're distributing needs to be stored somewhere. From what I've heard, there's no way it's at their clubhouse, so we gotta start narrowing down properties they have access to. Just didn't want to jump on him too soon after Jamie's accident."

"Your girl took care of Jamie," he replied. "No issues at all. They had her in for a follow-up yesterday. That darling girl is just fine. About now, I'm thinking he could use something to focus on besides reliving that shit."

I read the unspoken statement there that it was that exact reason why he was sitting in the sun with me. He'd nearly lost his granddaughter. For a while, that was going to haunt him. It was going to haunt us all.

"Speaking of your girl," he said, then lifting his chin toward the road.

There was that fucking car of hers. I know it was fixed, but every time I saw the damn thing, I pictured her stranded on the side of the road. I pictured that absolute devastation in her eyes when she'd first looked at me that night.

She'd never end up in that position again. I'd guarantee it. It didn't make my irrational hatred of that fucking car lessen, though.

"You gotta get her in a better ride," Roadrunner commented, and I huffed a laugh at how well it reflected my own thoughts. "We got a couple things moving through the garage that might be good for her."

"Been down that road, it doesn't end well."

He laughed. "So the sweet one's got some spirit, then?"

Did Evie have spirit? That was one fucking way to put it.

"Tried to tell her she wasn't moving out of the farmhouse yesterday," I informed him. "She's a tiny thing, but her attitude can fill the whole fucking place."

It had started by Evie telling me, excitedly to say the least, that she'd gotten a call from the local hospital asking her to come in today for an interview. Then, it had deteriorated fast.

"HOPEFULLY, I'll get a job there. The pay will be way better than the diner, so I'll be able to get my own place soon," she chirped, all smiles.

I was fucking thrilled for her until that. "Why the fuck would you do that?"

"I'm sorry?"

"Total fucking waste, babe, when I'd just drag your ass back to my bed every night."

Her expression had gone from pure joy, then confusion, and that had it swinging into anger fast. I wasn't the smartest man on Earth, but I was smart enough to know not to mention the way her nose twitched right through that transition, making it a hell of a lot less imposing than she was going for.

"Excuse me?"

I knew the old rule about women asking questions like that, that it was actually just an opportunity for you to change your answer. But she was talking complete bullshit.

"Why the fuck would you go through all the trouble and drop all that cash to get some fucking apartment, when there's no way in fuck I'm letting you sleep away from me?"

"You won't let me?"

Oh, she was gearing up, all right. "Take a second and really think about how asinine that plan is before you blow up."

The second those words came out, I knew they were a mistake. Even before her eyes widened like she couldn't believe I'd said it, I wanted to pull that shit back.

"Take a breath? You want me to take a breath and think about how asinine I'm being?"

Fuck.

Not good.

"Well, let me tell you, Mr. Badass Biker President. I didn't leave a life where I was under someone's thumb to end up there again. I swore the day I walked away from my parents that I would never, NEVER, end up in a position where I relied on other people to take

care of me. I was never going to be that powerless again. And clearly I failed at that, but that doesn't mean that just because we're together that I'm going to become the good little woman that lets you provide for me! Not ever!"

She'd started off all sass, and by the end, she was all out yelling.

"Bunny—"

"If that's not what you're looking for, if you want to be some… some…SUGAR DADDY, then I'm not the woman for you after all, because I refuse. I can damn well take care of myself!"

"Evie—"

"And another thing—" she started, but I grabbed her and slammed my mouth down on hers. Anything to get her to stop.

I pulled back, already having the words on the tip of my tongue so I'd get them out before she got on a roll again.

"I know you can take care of yourself. I know you could have found some man to take care of you a long time ago if you weren't that woman. Fuck, you could have stayed right where you were and had that financially.

"I don't want you for one minute not to go take that job. You should. You should do it because it's what you love and because I've seen firsthand that you're fucking good at it. I don't want you to stay here out of some fucked up bid for control over you. I want you here because I'm in love with you, even when you start irrationally screaming at me about shit. I've finally found the woman I want in my life and in my bed, and I don't want to crawl into it alone just so you can assert your independence.

"Now, you really need that, then we'll figure it out. If paying rent for an apartment somewhere feeds something in you that needs it, then

fine. I'll fucking deal. But if you're trying to do this just to make a statement about the fact that you're capable of doing it alone, then it is asinine. Not one fucking person here is questioning that."

We both stood there for a long minute, breaths labored a bit from the intensity.

Then, my sweet—if somewhat crazy, apparently—girl snipped, "Well, okay then."

SHE DIDN'T APPRECIATE that I started laughing at that, but she got over it pretty quickly when I introduced her to make-up sex despite her protests that we hadn't really fought that much.

It didn't matter; it was spectacular anyway.

"She has her moments," I said, watching my girl alight from that shitbox on wheels.

When she was out, dressed in a fitted maroon dress that had my dick responding, she threw her hands in the air and shouted, "I got the job!"

Fuck. She was so fucking cute.

I jogged to her, wrapping my arms around her middle and lifting her off the ground—which incidentally was when I noticed the heels she had on that would absolutely be staying where they were when I got her in bed, hopefully sooner than later. She laughed, bright and happy as I spun her once before dropping her back to the ground.

"Congratulations, bunny," I said, leaning in to kiss her.

"It's even in the neonatal unit. After one year, I can

hopefully move up to intensive care. After two years, they'll sponsor me to get a graduate degree," she gushed. "It's my dream come true."

"Your dream that you fuckin' earned," I corrected her, and she beamed up at me. "When do you start?"

"Monday," she answered, looking like she'd gladly drive back to the hospital and start right then if they'd let her.

"Good. Then I can take my girl out tonight to celebrate."

She gave me that smile that was brighter than the fucking sun. "I'd like that."

I started to lead her back to where I'd been sitting with Roadrunner, who was smirking like he found this shit funny, when I told her, "One condition."

"What's that?" she asked, looking up at me.

"You don't change out of that fucking dress."

She took another swing at my gut while Roadrunner got up, arms out, and said, "Congrats, girlie."

She went right in for the hug, thanking him. I unabashedly watched her ass under that fitted fabric. Oh, yeah, I was going to have some fun with that later.

"Should head inside, there are a few people around that'll probably all want to hear the good news," he said as she stepped away.

Evie looked back to me to make sure I would follow before she went through the front door.

Before either of us went after her, Roadrunner commented, "She's something else."

"Yeah," I agreed. That wasn't even the half of it.

"Happy for you, brother." He clapped a hand on my back, heading toward the door, where I could already hear a girly cheer rise up from whoever was hearing Evie's news.

Happy.

Yeah, that was the word. With her filling my life with her sweetness, I was fucking happy.

So I followed her inside to soak up some more.

CHAPTER 27
Stone

I WAS at my desk in the clubhouse, pouring over files. Jager hadn't just come through with my request for Devils's properties, he'd already compiled that shit on the first search. Not even ten minutes after I called him for that shit, I had it in my hands.

That had been three days ago. That night, the reconnaissance mission started. We were stretched thin adding that to patrols, but it had to be done. I'd been moving through the list of properties systematically. It wasn't just about finding out where they were packaging and storing their product, it was about knowing everywhere they might be, everywhere they had resources. It was about knowing our enemy inside and out before we made a move.

The last was why the list was staying in my hands, not being sent out to the Mayhem brothers. We weren't ready for them to go maverick with that intel.

They were antsy, as was evident by my phone ringing with a Portland number. Vic had gotten tired of Roadrunner giving him the runaround, so now this shit had stepped up to president to president. I'd been on the line with Vic three times in as many days, asking for updates.

Not even remotely in the mood to deal with that shit, I ignored the call.

Five fucking minutes later, it rang again. I didn't even look. That shit wasn't worth it.

I'd just made the final decision about where to send the guys tonight when the pounding started on the door.

"Yeah?"

Ham dipped his head in. "Daz called in. Says we need to get down to the club right now."

He didn't bother waiting, and he didn't need to. I was out of my chair, heading out right behind him. It was only on the move that I looked at the phone to see that second call had been Daz. This shit was fucking with my head so much I'd ignored him when something was going down.

Fuck.

Gauge, Slick, and Hook were outside mounting their bikes when I got there, each taking off without wasting time. I was right behind them, bracing for whatever was going to be thrown at us now.

Candy Shop was about a fifteen-minute ride from the clubhouse. We pulled into the lot in seven. The first thing that stood out was that the lot was empty. It was late afternoon, so the place wasn't open yet. But by now, most of the staff was usually in getting ready for the evening.

I swung off my bike next to Ham and asked, "He say anything about what we're walking into?"

"Nothin'. Just demanded we get our asses down here."

Not fucking good.

We made it through the doors, only to pause in the entry when we saw Daz in the middle of the floor, one of the bouncers tied to a chair in front of him. He didn't even turn to look at us, even though I knew he heard us come in.

"What the fuck is going on?" I demanded.

He didn't answer. Not right away. Instead, he reeled back and threw a punch right at the guy's jaw. It wasn't the first, not with the swelling and blood already on his face.

I closed the gap between us before grabbing my brother by the arm and ordering, "Explain."

The asshole in the chair was whimpering like a little bitch, and I heard Ham tell him to knock that shit off, but I was focused on Daz. He was practically fucking snarling as he stood there, getting his breath. The only other time I'd seen him so ready to lose it was before he beat the shit out of the guy that stole from Avery. The assault that I'd copped to.

"This fucking cunt," he snapped, an arm going out to the guy in the chair, who whimpered again, "brought this shit into my club."

He flung something small at me that I grabbed mid-air. I barely glanced at the insignia on the baggie before I passed it on. I didn't say a damn thing, but Daz caught the message either way. I wanted an explanation.

"Avery stopped by when everyone was getting in. One of the girls called her, asked if she could come by. She thought that shit was about helping with some moves. Turns out, she felt more comfortable telling Avery that this fucker offered her that shit, trying to fucking impress. She knew the score. She knew I don't allow that shit in here, and she said she wasn't interested in anything he was offering. Avery filled me in. She handled getting everyone else out while I got him out here to have a chat. Found that shit in his pocket."

I looked to Ham, nodding in the direction of the prick in the chair, but Daz shot up again.

"This one's mine."

Ham stepped back, hands up. Candy Shop might have belonged to the club, but it was Daz's brainchild. He had the idea, he put in all the legwork, he ran the fucking place on his own. This might have been bigger than blow in his club, but that shit still happened.

Daz wasn't waiting for my okay. He got back in that fucker's face, grabbing his jaw in an iron grip right where he'd landed the last blow. The cry he released only proved Daz's aim was true.

"Where'd you get that shit?" I asked.

Not seeming to grasp the severity of the situation, he just sat there whimpering. Daz, livid though he was, waited for my command. I gave him a jerk of my chin, and he threw a fist right into the asshole's stomach.

"I don't like repeating myself. I'll ask once more. You make me do it again, they'll be fishing a bullet out of your fucking leg. Got me?" He whimpered through a nod that probably hurt like a bitch with Daz's grip holding strong. "Where did you get the blow?"

"Some guy approached me at a party," he started, his voice trembling.

"When?" I cut in.

"A couple weeks ago? I don't know."

My eyes cut to Daz, who tightened his hand while he brought the other arm up, but he didn't get a chance to strike.

"Three weeks ago!" the asshole cried out. "Three weeks ago, Saturday."

"Who was he?"

He answered right away, wising up. "He went by Dog. He had a fucked up ear, and he wore a vest like you guys."

Dog was one of the Devils all right. At least there wasn't some other middleman to track down.

"You tell him where you work?"

Again, the answers came quickly. "Didn't have to. I went right there after work."

I watched as Daz's hand tightened reflexively. All the bouncers and bartenders wore shirts that had the Candy Shop logo on them. There was nothing wrong with that shit, even if he was thinking right then that there was. It would be something to address later. Much later.

"Where was this party?"

"Denning," he answered. Almost thirty minutes out of Hoffman.

Of all situations that could have led to this shit, it was the best. Odds were that bastard Dog stumbled onto the opening, took advantage. It wasn't set up.

That didn't do a damn thing to calm the fire in my gut, though.

"He tell you to sell it here? To go after the girls?"

The asshole's eyes got wide, and I had my answer before he stuttered out, "N-n-no."

No. It'd be what Dog was hoping for, but it was all on this motherfucker who thought he could look like a big man and get his dick wet.

"So you brought that shit here on your own accord? Onto Disciples' property?"

He looked about ready to piss himself, and I hoped like fuck he was at least that bit resilient enough. Nothing worse than some pussy making a mess someone had to clean up.

"I…I was…I mean…" He was too scared to form together a line of bullshit to feed me.

I flicked my eyes to Daz, who was all too ready to punch the fucker again, going lower this time.

"Mind the bladder, man," Ham put in on the same

train of thought as me. "We don't have a prospect anymore who gets the duty of cleaning that shit."

That was Ham, even in the face of shit like this, the brother had jokes. I didn't bother looking at Hook to see his reaction. The kid was made of ice.

I kept my focus on the little shit in the chair, trying to curl in on himself despite Daz's hold and the ropes. "You were thinking you would spend your work hours around a bunch of hot women that don't give you the time of day. You were thinking that shit you bought would make a difference. What you weren't thinking of was the warning you should have heeded when we took you on here. You don't bring that shit around. Not ever. You hear me?"

"Y-y-yes, sir." Still with the stuttering. It was hard to tell for sure with the sweat pouring off him and his face swelling up, but it sounded like he was crying.

Christ, I had no patience for this shit.

"Last question. You got a line to Dog? To get more of that shit?"

He shook his head, and Daz jarred him hard enough that I heard a crack before he screamed, "No!"

"No?"

He was definitely sobbing now, and I was done. Leaning forward, I shouldered Daz back and wrapped a hand around his throat. "Words, asshole. How were you meant to restock without a number for him?"

"The guys that own the house the party was at, they

have one nearly every weekend. He said if I wanted more, I could find him there."

There it was. The slow play, then. Get someone in our club involved, then make him come back for more. No hard approach, that was too likely to raise alarms. It was smart, surprisingly so for that group of brain-dead assholes.

I let go of the guy's neck, bringing my hand up to pat his cheek hard a few times, right where the worst of the damage to his jaw seemed to be, enjoying the little cries that accented each one.

Stepping away, I turned to look at my brothers.

"I'm done." They all knew what that meant. We'd been playing the waiting game, making smart moves to keep shit under control. No more. They'd targeted Candy Shop. Dog knew exactly what he was doing when he saw that logo. "Calling in Mayhem. This shit ends now."

"What do you want done with that fucker?" Gauge asked.

Daz was still staring him down, hands tight in fists, waiting for my order.

"Teach him a lesson that sticks."

I heard Daz crack his knuckles. "Anyone else want a shot before I finish up?"

I was already headed to the door but pulled up short when Hook spoke up. "Which girl?"

Turning, I noticed the tension in the kid, as if it weren't obvious in how he'd snapped the words.

"Candy," Daz answered.

Without a word, Hook stepped forward. The trained, lethal fighter Jager had honed was more than evident in the efficient, flawless blow he landed in the fucker's temple, making him slump unconscious against his bounds. Hook didn't linger, he walked right past me and out, the sound of his bike revving coming through the doors moments later.

"The fuck?" Ham muttered.

"Saw him talking to her at the party before that shit went down with Jamie," Slick put in.

"Asshole knocked him out," Daz bitched.

"You got your shots," Gauge pointed out.

"Not enough." Daz was right. Candy Shop was his, and he deserved to dish out retribution, but that last shot belonged to Hook.

"You'll get your shot," I told him. "At Dog."

The last thing I saw before I went outside to make the call to Mayhem was his sadistic fucking smile.

CHAPTER 28

Evie

I TRANSFERRED the little bundle in my arms to the waiting father, dutifully ignoring the tears in his eyes as he took his baby girl.

"Mind her head," I cautioned in a quiet, encouraging voice. Gently, I brought my hand to his arm, urging him into the best position.

"She's beautiful," he whispered in awe.

"She is," I agreed, but how fervently he felt that was far more so.

"Everything's okay?" he asked, worry masking his features.

"Everything looks great," I assured. "The physical exam yielded no concerns. We drew blood to run a couple screenings, and the doctor will let you know the results once we have those."

He blew out a breath, only to suck one back in and hold it when she started to cry. Across the room, the mother stirred at the sound.

"She's probably hungry," I explained, hoping to ease his mind. He nodded nervously and carried her over to his

239

wife. "Our lactation specialist is just down the hall if you'd like me to send her in."

Mom, already on alert, answered, "Yes, please. That would be great."

I offered them both a smile as I stepped out. Julia, who was in charge of overseeing me for the first few weeks, nodded to indicate I'd done well.

It was my third day on the job, and I was on cloud nine. There were times—they were rare, but they happened—when I'd wondered if I was pursuing the right path. I'd lain awake at night once or twice worried I wouldn't love the job as much as I'd hoped. Those fears had been largely dispelled during my senior practicum, where I shadowed a pediatric nurse practitioner, but starting here had truly laid them to rest.

The shifts were long, and I knew the hours would be particularly grueling when I had to do my rotation on nights, but every day was rewarding.

Luckily, Stone—being the biker boss he was—had the freedom to make his schedule what he wanted usually, so my time with him wouldn't be too decimated by my work. Even better, I knew he was the type of man who wouldn't begrudge me if it was.

However, based on the text I'd received about an hour ago from him, tonight wasn't going to be our night.

Stone: Club business came up. Don't know what time I'll

be back. Want you updating me when you leave there and get home.

It was terse, though I wasn't sure how to take that. I'd never texted Stone. It might be that he always sounded like that, but I worried the "club business" was more of the type that would have him pouring scotch—what I'd learned was his drink of choice besides beer—when he was done.

I also thought checking in when I left and got home was a little extreme, but I didn't mention it. More than once since we'd gotten together we'd had what I was now calling the "Evie's Car Discussion," this so coined because it began —on more than one occasion—with Stone stating, *"We gotta have a discussion about that car of yours."* This "discussion" began with how it was time to replace my car, moved onto how it was unsafe—at which point the argument "I found you on the side of the road, for fuck's sake," came up—and then ended with me none-too-sweetly explaining that since I apparently wasn't moving out, I'd get a new car after a few months with my new paycheck when I could afford one instead of taking one from "the garage" like he suggested.

Thus, I was feeling assured that his request for me to notify him of my movements was a not-so-subtle dig at my car. Since I'd rather avoid that topic, especially if he was going to get back late as it was, I let it go. Two texts might be ridiculous, but it wouldn't kill me.

"You did a great job today," Julia said after I'd spoken to Stacy—the lactation specialist—and sent her to the waiting couple.

"Thank you."

She checked the time, then told me, "You can go ahead and get out of here. I have to log your day before I get off."

I looked around to the clock behind the nurses' station, seeing it was ten to seven, and thinking I really needed to get used to checking my watch. I'd never worn one before, but it was a necessity of the job. In time, I'd get used to looking there instead of checking wall clocks or my phone.

"Sounds good. I'll see you Friday," I said, heading to the locker room to grab my things.

When I had everything and made the walk out to my car, I sent my obligatory text to Stone.

Me: Leaving work. XO

It wasn't until I was already on the road that I realized I had forgotten I wasn't heading straight home. No, I had to drive across town to the diner. Sal, the owner, was—for want of a better term—a douche. I knew for a fact he wouldn't be giving any waitress he hired to replace me my worn-out shirt or the stained apron, but he required me to return them, or he'd take eighty dollars out of my last check. Seeing as the aprons were cheap, bulky, unadorned ones and the t-shirt was about as low quality as they came, I was not about to let him charge me that much. He'd given me until Friday to return them, and my hope was that Stone and I would be able to stay in alone the next day. So, a trip to the diner it was.

I contemplated letting Stone know, but my phone was in my purse on the passenger seat, and I was firmly anti-texting-while-driving. It was a minor stop, even if it was out of the way. I'd just let him know when I left the diner.

The lot was mostly empty when I pulled up. Thinking about it, it should have been obvious that Stone was interested in me even if he said otherwise, if only because the food was terrible at the diner. Certainly not worth coming in as often as he did. Even if he didn't cook at all, there were better places to go in town.

Grinning to myself at the thought, I grabbed the uniform and got out of the car. Karen didn't bother to look up when the door opened. There was a dated sign that informed customers they should seat themselves, so she didn't feel the need to put in the effort to acknowledge anyone. She'd get to it when she felt like doing so.

I approached the counter, my eyes lingering on the seat Stone always took. I wouldn't miss this place, but I felt a pang of nostalgia for that chair. Not that the chair mattered much when I had the man it reminded me of next to me in bed every night.

"Hey, Karen," I greeted, forcing her to look up.

She popped her gum once, causing me to hide a cringe. I was glad there had always been only one waitress on at a time. I don't think I could have made it through a whole shift with Karen chomping away like she did. "Thought you quit," she said like I would be there in the middle of her shift to magically relieve her if I hadn't.

"I did. Sal wanted the uniform back," I explained. "He told me to just leave it with whoever was on."

She looked at it like she was going to claim taking the clean articles of clothing from me was akin to being asked to stick her hand in a medical waste bin, but she took the pile anyway. "What should I do with it?"

Rolling your eyes is rude, I could hear my mother's voice in my head. It was rarer and rarer it would happen, but now it grated on my nerves even more than whatever was irritating me.

"I don't know. Maybe just leave it next to the time clock?" I suggested.

She shrugged. Okay, then.

"All right. I'll...um...see you around." I probably wouldn't, but it was better than 'goodbye forever.'

"You working at the hospital now?" she asked before I could leave.

Frankly, I was shocked she remembered that piece of information about me. "Yeah."

She surprised me further by saying, in what seemed to be a truly genuine way, "Good for you."

Floored, I muttered, "Thanks."

She nodded, and I knew that was that. My one profound—all right, that might be an exaggeration—

moment with Karen, and right before we'd all but cease to exist to each other.

Bizarre.

My mind was still on the exchange as I stepped outside and approached my car. I can only imagine that was why I didn't notice him. Not until it was too late.

I heard him, too close, before I saw him. "Was thinkin' you weren't comin' in."

Wheeling around, I saw he was right behind me. He was big, nearly as big as Stone, and he wore a cut, too. But he wasn't one of the Disciples. I'd know it even if I hadn't met them all. The leer of his eyes, the crooked-toothed grin, the very lines of his body that brought him far too close to me all said 'creep.' No way he'd be let into the club.

I started to back away, wondering if I should make for my car or back inside the diner when he mockingly raised a gun from his pocket. "Now, now, gorgeous. Where the fuck d'ya think you're goin'?"

The hammering of my heart was so loud I couldn't think, couldn't concentrate enough to make a move.

"Here's what's gonna happen," he said, stepping in even closer until I could smell stale beer and cigarettes on his breath. "You're gonna come with me, or I'll fuckin' shoot you right in your pretty face. Don't really matter to me which one you pick. Get me?"

Since I didn't have much choice, I made myself nod.

"Good. And I'll add on, you scream, I'll shoot you before you can get a lick of attention. Yeah?"

Another nod.

"Good. Turn around and walk, bitch."

I did, following the pressure of the gun against my back to a beat-up van parked around the side of the restaurant. When I got close, he reached around me to slide the back open. I saw another man in the driver's seat for half a moment.

Then, there was a burst of pain in my head.

And blackness.

CHAPTER 29
Stone

I WAS SITTING in my office, palms pressed into my eyes.

Everything could go to shit fast now. The Mayhem Bringers would be rolling up anytime. When they did, it wouldn't be long before we rode.

The time there would be blood.

We'd made other choices before. We'd sacrificed that thirst in order to take someone down in a way that wouldn't have kickback for us. That wasn't an option now. Not one we could accept, anyway.

Still, I had to get on the line with Andrews, and there was no point in putting it off anymore.

At this point, I was just wasting time, but I couldn't help it. Evie would be getting off work soon. I told myself I'd just wait for her to text like I'd asked, then get down to it.

What was really happening was me taking a breath now, in the calm before the storm. Getting my head together to consider every outcome, every angle. Trying my best to make sure we were all breathing free when this was done.

I kept my head down, attempting to settle my mind until my phone vibrated.

Evie: Leaving work. XO

The XO in her message made everything quiet. That was the power she had, the power any good woman had for her man. Nothing soothed me the way she did.

I didn't reply. Not then. I'd give her something when she got out to the farmhouse. But hearing from her forced me to get my ass in gear. Closing out of my messages, I pulled up Andrews' number and put through the call.

"Tell me you're calling to get me to buy fucking cookies or some shit," he answered.

"Not waitin' around anymore," I answered.

"Just give me—"

"You don't need time," I cut him off. "We both fuckin' know they got the officers up there in their pocket. You aren't getting the chance to go after them anytime soon, and we aren't waiting anymore."

Andrews sighed. "You want to fill me in on what happened?"

Any other man with a badge, I wouldn't. Andrews had earned that honesty from us, though.

"They got that shit inside Candy Shop. Put it in a bouncer's hand, knowing full well who signs his paycheck."

He got it. I knew he would, but it was clear when he

muttered, "Shit. Fucking morons." He let out another sigh before asking, "How big a mess is this going to be?"

That was the question, wasn't it?

"We called in Mayhem."

Silence greeted that, then a harsh, "Fuck."

"You want to walk away, I'll respect that. You're willing to do what you can to keep my boys clear, you'll have my gratitude in all the ways you can. That includes whatever you need to make it happen."

It wouldn't be the first time he passed along incentives from us to folks that could make things messy for us. I meant what I said, though. If he wanted to remain far away from the shitstorm that was brewing, I wouldn't hold it against him.

Only a couple of men in the club knew how Andrews had come to be our ally. Only Doc, Tank, and Roadrunner were with me when I hunted down the scumbag that raped his little sister and gave him an opportunity at revenge that didn't involve her having to take the stand and relive that shit.

We might have spent a lot of time on different sides of the law, but Andrews knew what we stood for.

"I'll see what I can do," he finally answered. Before I could give my thanks, the line was dead.

Phone in hand, I let myself look at the picture Evie had taken of us with it. She'd even gone so far as to make it my background and lock screen. In the week or so since, she was surprised any time she saw it was still there. I wasn't changing it, not unless she jacked my phone again to take more.

Her smile. That was what I'd carry with me. We might be riding for our club, for Hoffman, for pride, and abstract bullshit. But I knew that wasn't enough.

"Every man that goes to war has to keep a picture in his mind."

I'd have Evie. A constant reminder that I had to get my ass home safe and without a warrant.

Pocketing the phone, I stood and made my way out into the clubhouse lounge. The brothers were all there waiting for instructions. So I gave them.

"I want everyone loaded up with whatever we got. Heard rumors about the fuckers stockpiling, so we aren't going in light. Women and kids go to the farmhouse. Full lockdown and I want volunteers to hang back and make sure they're good."

No one jumped up to raise a hand. I looked between the brothers with women and kids, the battle in their eyes between wanting to assure their safety and wanting to ride with their brothers.

My eyes moved to Jager, and he knew he was about to be benched since he had the youngest at home. Asshole wasn't having it. He spoke before I could, "Ace."

I looked between them. "Why?"

Ace answered that himself. "Quinn's pregnant."

Jesus. Too many families caught up in this shit. I looked to the other fathers with young ones. Gauge's expression was a challenge to sit his ass. Slick had much the same.

More than once he'd been the one to be sidelined since he'd be the first with a woman at home. For the look he was offering me now, it wasn't happening again.

That left, "Sketch," I announced.

His face didn't show it, but I knew he was relieved. He had two girls and a wife who'd already broken down once after losing her father when he wore our patch. He didn't need to be taking those risks.

"Get on the lines with your women now. I want them all at the farmhouse as quick as possible. You two," I said, looking between Sketch and Ace, "Arm up and ride up there now."

"Are Evie, Kate, and Owen there already?" Ace asked.

"Kate and Owen are," Daz put in. "Texted her a while ago. They're in for the night, told them to keep it that way."

I nodded. "Evie's on her way. She'll be there before you get up there."

Both men acknowledged that, then got moving. The rest of the club looked at me.

"I'm splitting you up. Teams for each property we haven't hit, and the one outside of town that we checked out already. My gut tells me the others don't matter. You go in soft with some of the Mayhem brothers at your back. Once we get eyes everywhere, we'll make moves. Got it?" With no protests, I moved forward, teaming them off and assigning properties.

Doc and Daz would be riding with me, Gauge with

Ham, Roadrunner with Jager and Hook, and Tank with Slick. It was calculated, and they knew it. Doc was like a father to Daz. Gauge and Ham were closer than any of the brothers. Roadrunner and Jager were bonded by Ember, and Jager had brought Hook in. Tank had been the one to recruit Slick. Everyone was tied to the men at their backs by more than just by brotherhood.

Should things go to hell, it could backfire on me. But I was hoping it meant everyone stayed safe.

The tension in the air was thick, like the charge before the bolt of lightning. The storm was on the horizon, whether we were ready for it or not.

THE ROAR of engines heralded the Mayhem brothers arriving, and then shit was full speed ahead. Teams were made, assignments reiterated. Everything was ready.

I was walking out of the clubhouse beside Vic, the brothers of our mutual clubs all ready to ride out, when my phone rang. I might have ignored it, but there was too much going on to take the risk.

"Yeah?" I answered.

"Pres…"

There was worry in Sketch's voice that sent ice through my veins.

"Talk," I ordered.

"Your girl. She's not here."

No.

My heart pounding, I ripped the phone from my ear, checking for anything I'd missed, but there was nothing. She hadn't texted to say she was home. She should have been back nearly half an hour ago.

I didn't bother with niceties. I hung up the call on Sketch and dialed Evie. I felt the eyes on me, the confusion, but none of it mattered.

The phone rang, and rang, and rang.

"Hi, this is Genevi—"

"Fuck," I bit out, slamming my finger down to disconnect and call again. The panic was rising. She was just driving. She stopped for gas. For dinner. She'd pick up if I kept calling.

"Stone," Vic called.

More ringing. That incessant fucking ringing.

"Hi, thi—"

"Brother, what's going on?" Doc asked, approaching the steps.

Nausea and pure fucking rage warred in me.

"Evie's gone."

Jager was sprinting past me in an instant, running inside the clubhouse. He'd track her phone, however far that got us. We'd find her. We had to.

I called again.

One ring, two.

Then a connection.

"Evie?" I demanded.

"Sorry, chief," a male voice said through the line. That chipper fucking tone making me grip the phone until the thing groaned its protest. "Your girl can't get on the line right now."

"Where the fuck is she?" I roared.

He chuckled. Fucking chuckled like I wasn't going to tear him apart.

"Now, now, so fuckin' pissy. She's fine." There was the noise of the phone moving around, then his voice more distant saying, "Take a look."

A minute later, my phone buzzed in my hand. With every muscle shaking, I lowered it. There, blocking the picture of her smiling face, was a small image of my Evie, bound and gagged in a chair. Her head was slumped forward.

"I'm going to find you," I said, not bothering to bring the phone to my ear. "I'm going to find you and rip you limb from limb. I'm going to make death feel like a mercy. And then I'm going to destroy your whole fucking club. Do you understand me?"

Everyone around me had gone dead silent, so I heard his response, even at a distance. "Good fucking luck. She's a sweet piece, your girl. Might have some fun with her before—"

My phone was gone then, slamming into the concrete exterior of the clubhouse.

I stormed into the clubhouse, heading right for Jager's room. He was there, staring at the screen.

"Tell me you fucking have her," I ordered.

"Signal just broke off," he said, still clicking away. "Probably busted the phone when you got off the line. I have a general location. Only two properties we know of are close." He turned the screen toward me, showing the map with a circle of Evie's location on it.

Marking the spot in my mind and comparing it to the maps I'd studied again and again of where they owned land, I went back out.

"Plan's changed," I announced when I cleared the door, shouting so all the guys would hear. "Those fucking cunts took my woman." There was a roar of fury, but I didn't stop. "We got a location, but it's not spot on. The two spots on the northeast side of town, about half an hour out. They've got her at one of those," I explained. "We ride now. We don't go in light. We get my woman out of there, and we do whatever the fuck we have to to do it."

That was it. I wasn't wasting more time on bullshit words. I heard Vic shouting orders for how to divide the men, but I was already getting on my bike. I tore out of the forecourt, opening my baby up full power.

"I have faith in this. I have faith in you."

Her voice was in my head.

"I want you to make love to me."

My sweet bunny, in danger.

"Morning, honey."

I was going to find her.

"My Stone."

And I was going to kill them for touching her.

CHAPTER 30

Evie

THERE WAS a vague sense of the world spinning.

My head felt…heavy. And overloaded. There was so much pressure.

And the spinning wouldn't stop.

I tried to open my eyes, but the light was so harsh, and it only made the dizziness worse.

Concussion.

Through the fog, that word hit me.

Right, a concussion. It explained the symptoms.

But how did I get a concussion?

My neck ached, and I realized I wasn't lying down like I should be if I'd been asleep—or unconscious? However long it had been, my head was hanging. I tried to lift it, but the wave of nausea stopped me.

"Well, look who decided to wake up."

That voice, it wasn't familiar. Was it?

It was hard to tell through the pain, pain that grew sharper the more I woke. It wasn't just the overall pressure headache; there was also a sharp, throbbing pain in the back of my head. Almost like I'd been hit there.

"Hey, bitch," the voice called again. "You fuckin' brain-dead now or somethin'?"

"Turn around and walk, bitch."

Oh, no.

No, no, no.

The man in the parking lot.

The gun.

He'd taken me.

The panic made me jolt, a feeble attempt to start fighting. My movements were uncoordinated, sluggish, and my head got foggier. But I had it together enough to notice the bonds, including the fabric tied across my mouth.

The nausea rose, choking me. I desperately swallowed it down.

What was going on?

Where was I?

What did they want?

A sob came out. I couldn't contain it through all the rest.

"Mmm. Scared and pretty. My favorite."

The bile burned my throat. I couldn't stop the tears, even as things grew disconnected.

Everything was too much. There wasn't enough air. The spinning wouldn't stop. My body was starting to shake.

Shock.

I was going into shock. I had to…

What?

What did I learn?

When did I...

Things were fading out. My body. The confusion. It all went away.

Except those noises.

Loud, familiar noises...

CHAPTER 31

Stone

I DIDN'T STOP.

Not when stoplights turned red on the way.

Not when I had to veer into the oncoming lane to get around cars in my way.

Not when the shitty old factory came into view.

I didn't give a fuck if they heard me coming. I didn't give a fuck if they knew I had a dozen men at my back. Let them get out guns and open fire.

At least then, if Evie was in there, she might have a chance.

No. Not a chance. Evie was walking away from this. There wasn't another option. I'd lay down my own life if I fucking had to.

Sure enough, the pop of gunshots filtered over the growl of engines. Knowing taking a bullet to the head wasn't going to fucking help Evie now, I swerved off into the tree cover beside the dirt road we were on.

I climbed off behind a big one, and everyone else split to both sides to do the same. I watched Sight, one of the

Mayhem boys, speed assembling a semi-automatic with a scope on the other side of the lane. He'd been an Army man, trained as a sniper. I looked at the building, catching movement but nothing clear enough to help me.

Sight whistled, loud and sharp. My head flew his way. He started gesturing, counting off bodies he could see. Three upstairs east, one west. Two coming from the front. I looked over and saw the assholes coming out and watched as Sight drilled bullets into both of them.

At least four more inside, probably more. Last I'd be able to get a number, the Devils were sitting at around an even two dozen. Every one of those assholes could be inside.

Vic patted my arm. I looked back to see him on his phone.

"They're at the other spot. My boy says there are at least ten guys inside. They're surrounding it and going in."

"They go in hard, but they do it carefully," I warned.

He didn't bother calling me on implying they'd do anything but. He stepped away, finishing the call. The second he hung up, I motioned to everyone that we were going in. I wasn't waiting, especially not now that they knew we were there.

Just hang on, Evie.

Sight hung back, doing his best to get a shot on the guys in the upper windows, forcing them to duck behind the walls instead of picking us off. There was no good in stopping when we were barging right in the fucking front door, so I didn't. Stepping right over the assholes on the ground, I burst in to see two guys coming at me armed.

I veered, keeping them from getting a clear shot even as the bullets flew. I fired at one as I recovered, clipping him in the knee and sending him staggering. Vic was right behind me, firing at the other. When he went down, I kept moving. Evie had to be here. She had to.

Another Devil came around the corner, but a bullet was already flying his way before I could adjust my aim. A glance behind me told me it was Slick who fired the shot. He and Vic stayed with me while the others fanned out, heading down a hall to the left and up the metal stairs. Instinct told me to forge straight on.

I didn't make it into the large, open heart of the factory before gunfire coming through the open double doorway forced me to take cover. But not so fast that I didn't see.

Evie.

She was there, tied up just like that fucking picture in the center of the room. All around was a mess of dilapidated equipment those cunts were hiding behind.

I felt steady. Despite the rage, despite the mortal fucking fear that she was hurt, my hands didn't shake. The adrenaline was a powerful thing.

Taking a half-second look around the corner before bullets hit the same spot, I clocked one of them. Vic had gone to the other side of the doorway, so I yelled to him, "Three o'clock!" He took a breath, then leaned around the corner to make the shot. An agonized "fuck" carried across the room.

It worked, but we could only hold out like this for so long, trying to pick them off from around corners when they knew where we were.

Taking a chance, I stuck my head out again before ducking back, focusing on the sound. Two shots, clear and loud against the distant din of gunfire and yelling. Could be someone didn't get a shot off, but more likely there were two left in the room, ready to fire.

"What do you want to do?" Slick asked.

What I wanted to do right fucking then was get to my feet and walk right in. Hopefully, I'd be able to get at least one shot off before those fuckers did, and one of the men with me could finish off the other. But it wasn't smart. It was a suicide mission.

"Pres?" Slick demanded.

I looked around more closely, seeing the hall behind him that must move around the exterior of the room ahead. I nodded that way, Slick's attention following my motion.

"Go. See if there's a back way in, get behind those fuckers, and take them down."

He looked reluctant. The brother probably knew where my head was at. If it was Deni in there, he'd be thinking the same fucking thing. He'd want to run in there, his own safety be damned if it meant she'd get out alive.

"Go," I commanded.

His jaw tightened, but he crept off. I watched him inspect around the corner, then disappear. I hoped to fuck I hadn't just sent him into a worse position.

I turned back to see Vic take another look. The responding shot hitting the corner of the opening before he'd fully cleared it.

"Can't see shit in there," he said, breathing heavy.

If Slick couldn't get around behind them, we had no moves.

"One of you cock suckers the one this bitch belongs to?"

My blood ignited like gasoline in my veins, but I made myself stay behind the wall.

"She's a really sweet thing, ain't she?" the cat kept shouting. "Nabbed her myself. Didn't even put up a fuckin' fight."

It made me fucking sick, but I knew Evie was smart. If she hadn't fought, it'd been because fighting would have gotten her hurt—or worse.

"It was too bad my orders were to knock her out when I had her. Might'a had some fun, she was still awake."

My grip on my gun started to hurt, the metal digging into my hand. Every muscle in my body felt ready to snap.

"Started stirrin' just before you fuckers got here. Thought I was going to get my chance to have a taste."

Every heartbeat felt like an echoed command drumming through my body. *Kill. Kill. Kill.*

"Stone," Vic warned, low.

"Maybe once we pick you assholes off, I'll keep her alive for a bit. Get myself a little sweet before I unload a clip in her."

Like fucking hell he would. I'd kill him with my bare hands before he'd be able to take me down. I'd bleed out knowing I did at least that.

"Hey, fucker!" he called again, trying to get me.

And then, he did.

Because the muffled scream that followed was one I'd never heard, but I knew right away.

Evie.

I didn't think. Not even for a second.

I was on my feet, charging around the corner in an instant.

He was there, in the middle of the room beside her. His hand was wrapped in her honey-colored hair, yanking her head up. Her eyes were hazy, unfocused. Her face that of pure agony.

And his gun was aimed at her chest.

"Well, well, well," he sneered, and I watched his buddy move through the room with a gun trained on me. "Looks like it is you, Stone."

"Put the gun down!" the other one ordered.

I didn't. Fuck him.

"See, Wrench had a special job for us," the fucker with his hands on Evie continued, also ignoring his partner. "He knew you'd come if we got your girl. Promised a ten grand bonus if we managed to take you without killin' you first."

I hoped that motherfucker Wrench wasn't at the other site. I hoped he was still out there for me to hunt down when this shit was over.

I wanted to be the one to make him scream before I put him down.

"Put down the fucking gun!" that other prick that was getting closer repeated.

I gave it a thought, counting back through the shots I'd fired. One bullet left in that clip. I couldn't take them both down.

Fuck it.

I dropped the gun to the floor, watching the one that asked for it flinch at the sound like a little chicken shit.

The slimy grin the first fucker gave me didn't do a damn thing to shake me. No, he had just the opposite impact when he turned his gun away from Evie to train it on me.

"That wasn't real smart, was it?" he mocked.

The fuck it wasn't. I got what I wanted out of it.

Evie was good. Vic was at my back to take a shot if they took me down. Somewhere in the bowels of this building, the Disciples and the Mayhem Bringers were taking down the rest of the crew that was here, a task I had every faith they'd manage.

They'd get Evie out, whether I was there to help or not.

I looked down at my beautiful bunny. Her eyes had dropped closed again, but her face was turned up toward me. I took in every feature, wishing I could have those eyes instead of seeing the streaks of her tears. Wishing I was seeing her smile instead of the gag on her lips. Wishing I'd done what I'd told myself I should two years ago and walked away instead of landing her in this hell.

If this was the price for that, I'd fucking pay. Anything to keep her from doing so.

It was only not wanting to see her in that state any longer that made me raise my head and see my opportunity.

Slick was sneaking through the room behind them, silent as the fucking dead.

I didn't keep my eyes on him, not wanting to give away his position. It'd all be about the timing. No, fuck that. It's all about fucking luck, but it was a chance.

Taking in a deep breath, I readied for it. To the cunt I'd shoot right now if any luck was on my side, it probably looked like I was bracing for death. Fat fucking chance. I'd never accept it so readily. Some motherfucker wanted to put me down, he'd have to take me down swinging.

The gunshot was my only warning. The instant I heard it, I dropped full speed to the concrete floor on my knees. A second shot went off right away, a reaction when the bullet hit. The jarring pain in my knees meant nothing. My only focus was getting my gun in my hand. A third shot, this one accompanied by an explosion of pain as it clipped my upper arm. It didn't even slow me.

When the cool metal was in my palm, I didn't bother aiming with finesse. I held my arm up, pointing high on that fucker, and took my shot. I watched with satisfaction as it hit right in that fucking asshole's throat, and he dropped.

I looked to my Evie, focused only on getting her out of there. We did it. We fucking did it. She was safe. She was…

She was bleeding.

At her stomach, there was a dark stain growing on her scrubs.

That second gunshot.

No.

"No!" I roared, barreling toward her.

"Stone?" I heard Slick question. A moment later, I felt him behind me and heard his hushed, "Fuck."

"Get her loose," I ordered, yelling even though he was right there. My hands were on her now, pressing against that wet warmth. I pressed in hard to try and staunch the flow while he did as I asked. Slick didn't waste time with the knots. He pulled out a knife and cut her free, breaking the rope again and again to get each loop free fast.

When her body started to slump toward me, I reached around her back. There was no exit wound. I didn't know if that was good or bad. All it meant in that moment was only having to hold one wound.

"Get Doc!" I heard the footsteps running away from the room. Vic running off to do that.

Doc was here somewhere. He'd know what to do to help her fast. The man had been a fucking surgeon. He'd save her.

He had to.

CHAPTER 32
Stone

WE SHOULDN'T HAVE TAKEN her to a regular hospital. Not with the questions they would ask. Not with two buildings littered with bodies that would burn any time now. But we'd had no other choice.

I knew from the second Doc arrived at my side that it was bad. Really bad.

He'd done everything he could, but we had to get her into surgery, and Doc didn't have the facility or tools to do it himself.

If I ended up in prison again, it would be nothing compared to her dying if she didn't get the help she needed.

We were sitting in the hospital waiting room. They'd taken her right in for emergency surgery and relegated me to a plastic chair to wait.

Her blood was still on me. I'd gone to wash it away, but it stained my clothes. It clung to the leather of my cut. I couldn't even see that. Just being in that bathroom and seeing it on my skin made me sick. Actually, physically fucking sick. It was a first that I could remember, but I took the thing off and handed it to Doc. Right there, agonizing as the minutes ticked by, I wasn't the president. I wasn't a Savage Disciple. I wasn't even Stone.

I was just Austin, and I could very well be losing the woman I loved.

My mind wouldn't stop churning over the images of the last couple hours.

Her bound to the chair.

The stain of blood forming on her shirt.

Having to stop holding the wound to carry her out to the van I was going to be eternally grateful someone brought.

Watching the ER staff wheel her away on the stretcher.

It was the worst nightmare I could imagine and every second was real.

I heard Doc on the phone at one point, giving orders to keep the club clear of blowback, talking to Andrews to see what he could do, arranging money to be sent to people with badges and who investigated fires. It was all my job, but it meant jack shit to me.

Eventually, I made myself speak though it felt like I'd swallowed glass.

"Can they fix her?"

"Stone..." Doc warned, but I wasn't going to listen to how I shouldn't think the worst.

"Tell me straight. Can they?"

He sighed, a sound that carried the weight of too many

years, too many patients on carts, too many that didn't make it.

"I don't know where that bullet went, what it hit. I can't say for sure without knowing that. What I do know is I've seen entry wounds in roughly the same spot where the patients survived. I also know the man in there operating. Two hospitals were possibilities to bring her to, I drove us here because I know he's the best bet."

That was something.

I wasn't even sure what hospital we were at. It hadn't mattered when we drove up and I'd been keeping as much pressure as I could manage on her wound. It had all been a rushing blur to get her through the doors. Now that things had all but stopped, there was nothing around but light wallpaper, tiles, and chairs.

"I'm not a praying man. Don't know you to be one either. But your girl is. Right now, you hope we're both wrong, and that girl's got some divine power on her side that'll see her through. You start making promises to whatever fucking thing out there you think might listen. You rage against the fucking Devil if that's what works. But you don't give up. You don't even think of giving up," Doc ordered.

I hadn't thought about God or prayer or anything like that since my mom passed. She'd believed. She'd brought me up with it, but it never really stuck. Doc was right, though. Evie believed. Evie had faith. I didn't have it in me to suddenly find that now, but I hoped for the first time that she was right. Because anything, God or man or fucking animal, that experienced her love would have to love her in return. It couldn't be helped.

I'd barely got a taste of what that was like, and I'd started falling.

She's going to be okay.

I chanted it in my mind, held onto every word. I couldn't give up. I wouldn't give up. Not because Doc told me not to, but because I knew they'd have to lower me in the ground before Evie ever gave up on me.

She's going to be okay.

She'd get better. We'd get all those days we should have. I'd fucking marry her, give her babies I knew she'd shower with all that love that poured out of her. I'd spend the rest of my godforsaken life getting to drink in all that sweet, and I'd never take a second of it for granted.

She's going to be okay.

There was just no other fucking choice.

"I love you, honey."

HER SKIN WAS PALE.

I couldn't stop looking at how pale she was without the rosy blush to her cheeks. I'd never noticed before that it wasn't just when she was feeling embarrassed. It was more pronounced in those moments, but it always colored her cheeks a bit.

At least, until now.

Now, without that color, without the light that seemed to shine out of every inch of her, she hardly looked like my Evie. Even the honey of her hair looked dull.

It'd taken hours to get her out of surgery. Hours of waiting until I was ready to rip that plastic chair they'd stuck me in out of the metal base and throw it. At one point, a nurse had forced me to go to one of the emergency bays to get the wound in my arm sewn up. I'd spent the whole time they cleaned and stitched the wound wanting to get back to that waiting room. Though, the second I was back, I remembered what torture it was to be there. At least the pain of the stitches had given me something to serve as a distraction.

The brothers had started to gather. Vic and the Mayhem boys stayed behind, taking care of business so the Disciples could be with me. No one forced me to acknowledge all that was going on beyond the walls of that hospital. No one even mentioned that shit to me. They'd handle it.

I wanted to appreciate that, but I was too numb to anything but my fear for Evie.

Ace and Sketch brought the women, who'd all tried to

get close and comfort me. It was only Avery who found a way. She didn't try to hug or talk or make promises that it'd be okay when she didn't know. She'd just sat beside me, close enough that I could feel her there. There was something steadying about that.

Maybe, when all this was over, I'd find the words to thank her.

Maybe, if I made it through this, I'd find a way to thank them all for being at my back.

Right now, though, I focused on her pale fucking face, and I started talking.

"Three days. It's been three days since I saw you smile last. I'd give anything for that sweet, beautiful smile to be on your face now." There was no smile for me now. There was no expression at all on her face. "I wouldn't even need a smile. Just to see your eyes, or see that fucking nose…"

The words got stuck in my throat, my gaze fixed on that pert nose that didn't wiggle now.

"If you could hear me, I'd tell you how I should have left that day in the diner when you asked me out. Not for good like I'd thought, but I should have walked out and gotten you a fucking ring. I should have put that thing on your finger and tied you to me in any way I could.

"I'd do it now. In a fucking heartbeat, I'd get you the ring, the dress, whatever the fuck you wanted. We could do it in a church for all I cared. I'd drag you there right this minute if I could and give you those vows."

Evie didn't respond, but I knew she wouldn't. How could she?

"There was a time I'd have thought it'd be hard to get all the brothers into a church to share that shit with us, but it'd be easy. They wouldn't even hesitate because you made them all love you, too.

"Biggest fuckin' problem we'd probably have would be all the women wanting to stand with you. I'd have to put half the club up at my side to even shit out, and then we'd have damn near no one in the seats watching.

"Funny how that shit doesn't seem like a problem at all."

It wouldn't be. Nothing would be a problem if I was swearing forever with Evie. The fucking sky could come crashing down around us and it wouldn't matter.

Reaching out, I took her left hand in mine, hating that she didn't hold me back.

It wasn't a new feeling. I'd been living that hell for three days. The paleness, the silence, the agony that was not having my Evie.

The doctors had managed to find the bullet. They'd called it a near miracle that there had only been the minimal damage to the organs it grazed. Even a centimeter in any direction, it would have been a very different story. Still, they could offer no guarantees. They would monitor everything closely and see what her body did next.

Hour after miserable hour passing in that hospital room. My Evie in a coma, machines beeping away to monitor her, meds pumping through her system to heal and to keep her sleeping. The last had ended yesterday. They'd made no guarantees about when she might wake, but it could be any time.

Except it didn't happen.

I never left her bedside more than a couple minutes to use the restroom. I didn't even eat since I couldn't bring food into her room. Hunger wasn't even a thought. Being there if she woke outweighed anything. Even sleeping seemed insignificant.

"Please, Evie," I pleaded, barely noticing the tubes and wires anymore. Just that pale, expressionless face. "Wake up for me, and we can have all that. Whatever you want, I'll give, bunny. You just have to wake up."

There was nothing in response, and I felt the weight in my gut, heavier each minute she slept on. I didn't know how to say goodbye. Fuck, I wasn't convinced I could.

I didn't have more words to give her. Not then, not with that fear. Instead, I did what I'd been doing for days. I got out my new phone. Someone had replaced it for me so I could reach anyone I had to, though it didn't matter since they were all still camping out in the hospital in shifts.

When I got it, I'd starting downloading songs. Anything I could remember her singing, anything I could think of that she might like. I played them for her while she slept. I knew how much that music meant to her. I liked to think it comforted her to have it.

I hit play, resuming the shuffle where it stopped before.

The one that started was a song I added. I didn't know if Evie knew it. It was one my mom liked when I was a kid. I knew the version I found wasn't the original, but the woman singing reminded me of Evie. I let Cat Power sing "Sea of Love," and I held her hand. There was nothing else for me to do now.

It was in the middle of the second verse when it happened. Her hand moved a bit.

My ass was out of my chair in a fucking second, leaning over to run my fingers across her temple.

"Evie, bunny, I'm right here," I called. "You're okay. Just wake up and show me those eyes."

Her lids started to twitch, and I couldn't fucking breathe. There was no air left as I watched them flicker again and again. And then crack open just a bit.

"Evie. My sweet girl," I choked out, not giving a fuck that there were tears forming. Not giving a fuck if she saw them. She was waking up. She was coming back to me.

It wasn't fast. Her eyes would peek open slightly, just to close again. When the song came to an end the first time, I'd fumbled with the phone, managing to get my shaking hands to put the song on repeat. It was just a coincidence. Some part of me knew that, but I wasn't taking any chances.

Almost an hour later, I was looking into brown eyes. They were hazy and a bit scared as I explained that she was all right, that she was in the hospital, that she'd been hurt.

"But it's going to be okay," I promised. She was awake now so it fucking would be. "We're going to get you better, bunny."

She made a feeble attempt at lifting her hand, so I brought it up to my face like she always did. I was a mess, an absolute fucking disaster, but that touch centered me as it did every time.

"I love you, Evie."

Then my girl—*fuck*, my girl—she looked right at me.

And her nose twitched.

CHAPTER 33
Evie

I WAS AT THE STOVE, making French toast. The simple task was draining, and I knew I'd have to lay down again soon. I'd probably have to eat the meal off of the tray I'd come to despise while in bed. At least I'd been able to get up and do this myself, though.

For the last several weeks, Stone had been doing everything for me. This one little thing was something I could do for him.

I flipped the two slices in the pan, humming "Sea of Love" as I did. My memories of those first days after I woke up in the hospital were foggy at best. Stone had told me since that I'd completely forgotten about having woken up before the first few times, or that he'd already told me why I was there. None of that had stuck. Hearing him talk about it felt like listening to a story about a stranger.

The one thing I did remember, though, was that song. I'd asked him to play it for me more times than I could count while I was stuck in the hospital bed. When I started having more visitors and Avery showed up with a replacement for my phone, I'd downloaded it for myself.

What happened to my phone, I didn't know. At least, not specifically. I didn't have much in the way of specifics about what happened from the time I was taken to the time I woke in the hospital. The only details I knew for sure were the medical ones. I'd read my chart and spoken to the surgeon myself about that. I understood precisely what my recovery was going to look like—which also meant I knew that I was pushing it a little that morning, but I was stir crazy.

The rest I didn't ask many questions about. Maybe at some point, when I was more healed and looking back on this, I'd need to know. Stone had promised he would give me everything if I asked, but I hadn't. In part, that was because I could see every day how much it was weighing on him. I understood enough to know what happened was related to the Disciples and Stone was feeling at fault. The last thing I wanted was for him to relive it all right now.

As for me, I didn't blame him. I didn't blame the club. I knew they'd put themselves on the line to save me. Having lived most of my life surrounded by people who barely made an effort to show they cared in the easy times, I appreciated as much as anyone the sacrifice they were all making doing whatever they did to save me. Those men had families at home, but they'd put themselves on the line. Whatever came before, whatever happened that might have led to me being caught up in it, that didn't matter.

His footsteps carried through the hall and into the

kitchen before his arms closed around me carefully, only touching up at my ribs, but I focused on breakfast.

"Why are you out of bed?" Stone asked gruffly into my neck.

"I'm making breakfast," I pointed out the obvious.

Stone wasn't amused. He never was when he thought I was being a risk to my recovery. My say on the matter didn't hold much weight. It was a big part of why I'd become so stir crazy. "You could have woken me up and I'd have made breakfast."

That was true. If I so much as shifted noticeably while he slept, Stone was ready to jump out of bed and do whatever I needed. Hence why I'd taken advantage of the fact that he'd somehow slept through me getting up to use the bathroom this morning.

"I'm fine, honey. It's important at this phase of recovery that I start moving more," I reminded him.

On a grumble, he shot back, "I don't give a fuck. You're going to overdo it."

My sweet, temperamental, overly-cautious biker. I removed the last pieces of French toast from the skillet, flicked off the burner, and turned in his hold.

"How long am I going to be handled like fine china?"

Oh, yes. He was grumpy. The lines segmenting his face made that perfectly clear.

"You'll be lucky if it's not your whole damn life, bunny."

I rolled my eyes. We both knew that wouldn't be true.

Eventually, he would adjust. Heck, at some point he wouldn't have a choice. I would go back to work when my body could handle it. I was floored at the understanding from the hospital when they learned what had happened. In that mysterious biker president way of his, Stone handled the whole situation in a way that didn't come back to the Disciples. By extension, in the eyes of the law and my superiors at the hospital, I was only a victim of a tragic situation, not the woman of a dangerous biker. They couldn't give me paid leave for as long as my recovery would take, which I understood, but my position was saved —though it might require a movement between departments to pediatrics or something else for a period of time depending what staffing was like at the time—when I was ready to return.

It was tough not to dwell on my dream taking a little longer, especially when my days were spent stuck in bed. However, it did help that I was rarely left to entertain myself. Stone was nearly always at my side, and the whole of the Disciples family was coming around as much as they could. Even Jager came twice, once without Ember with him. He did bring Jamie, though—which I was thankful for since I didn't quite know what to say to the surly, quiet guy. I appreciated him making that effort either way.

I appreciated everything they were all doing for me, even if I wished it weren't necessary.

"You can carry all the food upstairs," I offered. He raised an eyebrow that told me my effort to placate him didn't work. He'd have carried the food up whether I granted permission or not. I took a few steps around him to the cabinet to grab another plate, and the fatigue of the morning hit me hard. "Actually, you can carry me upstairs if you want to, too."

There was scarcely time for me to set the plate down before Stone was picking me up. It was fast, but it was exceedingly gentle so as not to jar my healing core. "I fuckin' knew you were doing too much."

I wouldn't admit it out loud, but he might have been right. It was a part of the process, though. I wasn't in considerable pain, just tired out. I'd have to experience that a lot to get my stamina back.

Stone settled me in my familiar spot on the bed. His whole room had been transformed since before my injury. All of my things had been moved in, pictures of us and our friends had been framed on the walls, and everything had been outfitted to make life easy for me. Someone had gotten a table that could easily wheel up to the bed and be adjusted to different heights across my lap, which Stone situated after I was good to put my food on. He then jogged back out to go grab our breakfast.

It was later, when we'd finished eating, and I was in an endless scrolling session, trying to hunt down a new show to watch—and thinking I might need to text Quinn, who seemed to have a bevy of shows she recommended, not to mention all the books she'd been bringing—when Stone spoke.

"I'm calling the brothers in for church tomorrow," he said, and I nodded. He always kept me updated on his schedule so I could find someone else to come hang out with me if I wanted.

"Okay, honey," I responded, still clicking away on the remote.

"Gonna call for a vote."

"A vote?"

He didn't clarify for a long moment, and when he did, I couldn't believe it. "I'm giving up the gavel."

"I'm sorry, what?"

"I'm stepping down as president."

"You can't do that!" I cried, sitting up fully. Then, I was crying out again at the sharp pain the movement caused.

"Evie, Jesus," Stone muttered, leaning in to help me settle back down.

"That was your fault," I argued. "How could you even say you're going to give up being the president?"

He didn't meet my eyes when he answered, "That's the fucking problem. A lot of shit is my fault."

Oh, okay. I needed to tread lightly here, but him thinking that way couldn't go on. It was the elephant in the room we'd been studiously avoiding, but there was always a point when it made its presence known.

"Honey," I called, but his head stayed down. His hand was on my side, not far from the spot where I'd been hit. "Stone," I tried again, but he didn't look. "Austin."

That got me his eyes, their stunning gray depths painted with sorrow and regret.

"You didn't do this to me," I started. He was going to protest, or just tell me we weren't going to talk about this now because I needed rest, but I wasn't about to let that happen. "You didn't. Not in any estimation. I know I don't know all the details, but those men that…" I had to swallow down the lingering fear thinking about it drummed up to continue, "that took me, they were causing other issues with the club, weren't they?" He didn't respond, but not disagreeing was answer enough. "Club business is club business, but that doesn't mean the women don't talk. I know who the Savage Disciples are. I know that sometimes you all have to do things to protect us or to take care of this town. Whatever was happening, I know it wasn't just about something silly.

"You all were standing up for a reason, and from what I've come to know of the club, it was probably a reason I'd have been glad you were up in arms about. You feel guilty that they took me to use against you, but don't you think I know that things could have ended very differently? Don't you think I realize that you risked yourself to get me out?"

His jaw tensed, and I knew I was right. Stone had voluntarily gone to prison to keep his club brother free. He'd denied himself what he wanted because he thought it was better for me not to be with a man his age. When they took me, I didn't doubt for a minute that he'd have willingly done whatever was necessary to get me free—even if that meant giving up his own life.

It was a realization I'd been dancing around in my head for weeks. When it came to mind, I forced it away because it was too much to bear.

"I love you," I told him, tears making my eyes and nose burn as they made my voice tight. "It isn't your fault that there are terrible men out there that would do what they did. It's not your fault that they used me against you. The same thing could have happened if you were a police officer. Would you be thinking about giving up your job then?"

His fingers danced across the place where the bullet had hit. "Evie." His voice broke on my name, and he cleared his throat. "They shot you. They took you and tied you up and fucking shot you because of me, because I'm the president and they wanted to fuck with me. I won't ever have you in that position again."

"So, who steps up then? Roadrunner? He's got a daughter and granddaughter to consider. Tank? Gauge? They both have Cami and Levi. Sketch? Slick? Daz?" I kept pressing, even as he shook his head. "Every Disciple has people they love. Even if we take away the women and kids, you still all have each other. You guys tried to protect us all. I went off on my own, not thinking about the fact that there was a reason you wanted to know where I was and when. But it's not my fault, and it isn't your fault or the club's. The only people at fault are the ones who did it. And you made them pay. The whole club made them pay."

That was part of the story I didn't know, not wholly. Stone had only made it clear that retribution had been delivered. Honestly, no matter what time passed, I wouldn't want to know more than that.

"I don't want you to give up your place leading the club," I went on. "Your brothers won't either. And I don't think you want to, not really. Being the president is who you are. Don't let them take that from you."

For a long time, he didn't say a thing. He sat close, holding my eyes with his. There was a war there beneath the surface that he needed to fight. My man was strong, though. I knew he'd defeat those demons in the end.

"Maybe I'll wait a while," he finally conceded, and I felt a small smile forming on my lips.

It was a victory. A little one, maybe, but still a win.

"Then, I have more time to convince you."

He kissed me. It was soft like they all were now. I missed the others, the passionate ones that set me on fire, but they would only lead us to a road we couldn't take. Not yet.

"How about forever?" he asked when he released me.

There was nothing small about the smile I gave him then.

"I can do forever."

CHAPTER 34
Stone

FOUR MONTHS LATER

"WHAT THE FUCK do you mean you were going to step down?" Ham demanded.

"Are you shitting me?" Daz tacked on.

Those two were the loudest, but there was a mess of the same shit coming at me from all sides.

"All right, shit." I tried to shut them up, like that was going to work.

"You'll be lucky if we even let your ass retire from that shit when you're old as fuck like Doc," Daz kept right on.

"Fuck you," Doc shot back.

I banged the gavel hard, making my point a little clearer.

"Did any of you fuckers catch that I said 'was?' Shit."

Tank asked the question that I knew was just going to incite them more. "How long were you thinkin' that shit?"

Fuck. Here went nothing. "Four months."

Only, I didn't get a bunch of bullshit handed to me. I

got silence. Everyone knew exactly what happened four months ago, what triggered that for me.

"What changed your mind?" Roadrunner, who knew I'd have nominated him for my job, asked.

"She did."

Evie had made it her goddamn mission. I think she'd been more committed to that than her own fucking recovery. What really made it through wasn't one of her attempts, though. It was about a month before. I'd woken in the middle of the night, images of her in that fucking chair hounding me, and my startling awake had jostled Evie.

"HONEY?" she called, her voice heavy with sleep. Any other time, it'd make me hard hearing that. Right then, having just woken from a nightmare of being back in that factory, of my girl still in those cunts' hands, all I could feel was the desire to trade my soul to bring one of those fuckers back and kill them again.

When I didn't respond to her, Evie sat up gingerly and moved in close. Her delicate hand came to my sweat-soaked back, but she didn't recoil.

"Talk to me."

I promised her—promised myself—that there was no more keeping her out. Not out of my head, not out of my life. There may be times I'd have to keep club shit quiet, but never again if it even might involve her.

"Go back to that night a lot. In my sleep, but they aren't normal

nightmares. Nothing changes. It just plays in my head again, like I never got you out. Like I'm still just standing there wondering what the fuck I'm going to do to save you."

Her silk lips kissed my shoulder, then her forehead rested there. Her hands wrapped around my arm, hugging it to her torso, and I brought my hand to her bare thigh. She didn't say anything, just held onto me like she could absorb that shit out of my skin.

It was only then for the first time that I realized this situation hadn't been reversed.

"You don't dream about it?"

Her head jerked like she'd never thought of that either. "No," she answered, her tone surprised.

"Not at all?"

"Not at all." She kissed my shoulder again. "I don't really remember it. I can remember when they took me, though even that's a bit unclear. After that, it's all just blank until I was in the hospital."

I'd think that would make it worse, that the mind could think up all kinds of shit to fill in those blanks.

"I guess," she went on, "I just have the very beginning and the end. I don't have the horror of the story in the middle. All that's there is knowing you saved me, so that's what I focus on."

That fucking simple. Her body was healing, and she was just letting that shit go, while I stayed in that room to fucking rot.

"I want to let it go."

She gripped me tighter. "Then let it go, honey."

"I don't know how," I admitted.

"I don't either, not for you. You have to know why you're holding onto it. If you can get past that, the rest will solve itself."

THAT WAS IT. Those words. Because I already knew
why I was holding onto it. It was the guilt that kept me
there. If I wanted to leave, if I wanted to keep from
waking in the middle of the night and dragging her back
there when she was leaving on her own, I had to
acknowledge that it wasn't in my power to control
everything. I couldn't control the fact that sick
motherfuckers like that existed in the world. I couldn't
change that they pushed us until we had no choice but to
take them on. If we hadn't, worse could have happened
to all of us eventually, including Evie. In time, they'd have
pushed themselves right into Hoffman. Or even if they
hadn't, others would have seen the foothold they got and
made the same moves. Fuck knows what might have
gone down.

It wasn't like that change happened overnight, but I
grappled with it. Evie cheered me through. And after some
time, the nightmares slowed. I had them occasionally,
maybe I always would, but they weren't controlling me like
they had been at first.

"Fuckin' knew I liked that girl," Daz kept running
his mouth.

"Anyway," I pressed on, ignoring him. "I'm bringing
that shit up because I decided not to, but only if no one
else wants to take the gavel. Someone else wants it more,
I'll step aside."

Not one of them even looked like they were considering it. Then, Roadrunner stood.

"All right," I started to say that he could have it. He'd been a great VP and had handled everything while I'd been inside anyway.

He spoke over me. "All in favor of keeping our pres right where he is?"

Every brother voiced their "Aye" right away.

"Good. Then that's the last of that shit," he muttered, dropping into his chair again.

My club was a bunch of assholes, but I loved every one of those fuckers.

EVIE WAS on the couch at the farmhouse when I got home. It was a shitty thing to think, but part of me missed those hours in bed. I didn't miss for a fucking second the pain she'd have, but being able to escape to bed with her all day was just fucking fine, even if there was none of the good shit that happened in bed going on.

"How'd it go?" she asked, and I just gave her a look.

She'd had a doctor's appointment, which she

conveniently didn't tell me was at the same time I'd called the brothers in for until after. This was so, she said, she'd have a different "babysitter" who wouldn't be on her case so much.

I called it a bunch of bullshit.

"My appointment was fine." She gave me what I was looking for. "He said I'm recovering remarkably well, and I'm free to resume all my normal activity as long as I'm aware of my body and take it easy if need be. He wants to wait another few weeks before I go calling the hospital to get back to work, try out being active for even half that long before going back to twelve-hour shifts, but otherwise, I'm good."

I bent down, pressing a kiss to her upturned lips. "That's good, bunny."

"Mhm. Now, how did it go today?"

Kicking back on the couch beside her, I explained, "Good. Told them I'd considered stepping aside," which I'd already told her I was planning to, "they were pissed. Roadrunner ended up calling a vote to keep me where I was."

"And?" she asked it like I was about to tell her if the last number on her ticket won her the jackpot.

"Fucking unanimous."

Her smile was big, fucking huge actually. The sweet girl she was, she didn't even gloat.

She just leaned into me and gave me a kiss this time. "Mr. President," she teased. "So it's good news all around."

"Yeah, babe." It was starting to feel like every day would be that way with her.

"We should celebrate."

There was a light in her eyes that made my cock stir. The all-too-familiar battle against that feeling against the constant desire she had boiling beneath my skin began to wage. Her wellbeing was more important than the fact that my cock ached, more important than shooting off in the shower every morning was dissatisfying. More than once— a fuck of a lot more than once—Evie had tried to ease the ache. I wouldn't let her. One-sided shit with her would only make things worse, only make me want her more. Even besides that, my girl wasn't going to service me without getting her own back.

Despite all that, my fucking mouth worked before my brain. "What did you have in mind?"

I had to dig my fingers into her soft thighs to keep my hands from wandering. It was pathetic, my complete loss of control with her.

"I think you're more equipped to get creative than I am." She batted her lashes, a seductive move that contrasted against the rose of her cheeks in a way that owned me.

"Evie." It was a warning, the same one I'd been giving for weeks since she'd started feeling well enough to test me.

She leaned in, lining up her lips with my ear, her tits pressing into my chest. "The doctor said I can resume normal activity, honey. *All* normal activity."

Not even a second ticked by after those words rocked through what felt like my whole body before I was on my feet, Evie in my arms. Her joyful giggle and the answering growl it brought out of whatever fucking beast I'd become trailed us as I took her upstairs.

I didn't see the stairs, the hallway, even our room. The only thing that could hold my attention was my beautiful Evie, her brown eyes bright with mischief even as they darkened in a way that called right to my cock. It was instinct born of living in that house for years that led my feet where I needed them to take me, that I managed to shut the door behind us.

"I missed you." Her words were like a confession as I lowered her to the bed. My dick throbbed his agreement in kind as if she'd said the words to him. Though, maybe she had. She'd had all of the rest of me over the months of her recovery.

There might have been words that a different man would give her in response, flowery shit to make her swoon, but I wasn't that man. I was the man who needed her, down to the fucking marrow. Words were most of what I could give her for months, now they were bullshit. She owned me, and there was no better way to show her how much.

Mindful of her injury—recovered or not—I pulled her yoga pants off of her. Jeans had been too difficult, so my girl had taken to wearing those ass-hugging things all the time. I was convinced it was at least in part because she knew how much the sight tortured me. If I didn't think she'd flip out right then, I'd have ripped right down that seam at her pussy and fucked her with the remains where they were. At least one pair would be toast then.

All thoughts of pants, or anything but this moment, fled when I saw the wet spot darkening the pink fabric cupping her pussy. Months I'd been without that sweet, and here she was, ready for me to take it again. Unceremoniously, I pressed my knuckles against that beacon, rubbing deep and firm, feeling the heat seeping through.

"You need it." *I* needed it.

"Yes." Her hips rolled, trying to get me deeper despite the barrier.

"What do you need? My fingers?"

She shook her head, eyes wide, mouth open to allow her panting breaths.

"My mouth?"

She started to shake her head on instinct but froze. Then, either without thought or in a coordinated move to decimate me, she licked her lips.

Mouth it fucking was then.

Her panties were gone in the work of one movement, and her hips were scarcely able to settle back onto the bed before I was bent between her legs, taking one long lick up her soaked pussy.

"Stone!"

Her hands were in my hair, gripping it to the point of

pain, but I couldn't give less of a shit. I worked her with my tongue, reveling in the feeling of having her sweet cunt back. It was building in her, her hips thrashing, her pussy clenching, her cries echoing in my ears. I was going to take her over the edge, and then I was going to bury myself inside her until I couldn't get it up anymore.

Except, that didn't happen.

"No," she cried, the word more of a moan from the last roll of my tongue. "With you. I want it with you."

There was no way I could deny her that.

"Shirt."

She followed the growled command without hesitation, losing the top and her bra to boot as I ripped my own clothes off. The fucking things were just in the way.

Evie welcomed me back onto her with arms and legs open, letting me fall right into place where I belonged before wrapping me up. With her under and all around me, the scorching wet of her pussy kissing my aching cock, I found I did have words.

"This is heaven. Just this, with you. Not one fucking thing could ever top this."

Anything she might have said was swallowed by her cry as I thrust in, sliding home until my whole cock was buried deep.

Home. That's what it was. What anything with Evie to me was. My sweet bunny was home, was everything.

And just like her, just like she'd done every time I'd thought she couldn't possibly top what she'd already given me, Evie gave more. In the midst of that cunt squeezing me tight, spasming as she came for me, right when the sensation of it was about to make me blow, Evie turned her head toward me. Months built of lust, of self-doubt, of guilt and sorrow and anger, disappeared as I came with her rasped "I love you" in my ear.

CHAPTER 35
Evie

EIGHT MONTHS LATER

"BY THE TIME I pop out this kid, I'm going to be the size of a house," Avery griped, but still took another bite of the chocolate cupcake she'd just grabbed.

I swallowed my laugh. At four months, Avery was definitely eating for two. Since half that food came from her bakery, she seemed to always be snacking on some sort of dessert.

"Don't worry, sugar," Daz assured, his grin making me brace for whatever depraved thing he might say next. "Just more cushion for the pushin'."

Yes, there it was.

Avery swung out and hit him in the stomach. Unfortunately, she did this with her cupcake hand. A smear of chocolate mocha frosting covered Daz's cut, and her face dropped.

"My frosting," she pouted.

I was about to get up and grab her another one when Daz said, "You can lick it off me."

With that, I decided the safer option was to just exit.

Daz's mouth and Avery's pregnancy mood swings were proving to be an explosive combination. I also knew—though part of me wished I didn't—that the hormones were causing her to experience other symptoms that made those arguments get heated in a completely different way nearly every time. If it weren't for a year of hearing Daz say things like that all the time, I might have thought he was just trying to get a rise out of her to get her in bed.

Heck, what did I know? Maybe that was part of their dynamic from the start.

I walked across the clubhouse yard, taking it all in. Summer was grabbing hold of Hoffman, and for the Disciples, that meant as much time outside as they could get. That afternoon, they'd gotten a whole mess of meat to smoke. Everyone was there, including the two new prospects who were—as usual, I was learning—charged with any little task around. For the moment, that meant keeping everyone's drinks topped off.

It'd been over a year since these people had become my family, and it was already hard to imagine a time that they weren't. The way they all loved, the ferocity of it, was something I couldn't bear to lose now.

Not that I was worried I ever would.

"Aunt Evie!" I heard cried out and saw Emmy running my way, fake stethoscope around her neck. For the moment, she was convinced she wanted to be a nurse someday like me. Since this changed every couple weeks—

except princess, that career was constant—I wasn't getting too attached to the idea. Still, it was nice to have her be my little shadow for the moment.

"Nurse Emmy," I greeted, kneeling down. "Have you treated any patients today?"

"Yeah. Lina hurt her arm, so I gave her bandages to make it better." Lina was her younger sister, Evangeline, soon to be the middle child since Ash was pregnant again.

"Eighteen bandages," Sketch clarified, coming by and lifting up his daughter, who was all too willing to be the center of her daddy's attention. My eyes widened, and he just shook his head. "Unfortunately, Mommy gave Lina a bath and they all came off."

Yes, I'm sure that was very unfortunate. Though, it was better than a couple months ago when Emmy was insisting she was going to be a tattoo artist like her dad and colored all over her sister. That didn't clean off as easy with one bath. Washable markers, it seemed, might be an overstatement.

"I fixed my boyfriend Kyle at the park the other day, too," Emmy offered, not catching on to her father's sarcasm.

Sketch froze. "Your what?"

"My boyfriend," she supplied, helpfully.

I pinched my lips together. Apparently, leaving Daz and Avery behind was an out of the frying pan into the fryer situation.

"Firefly!" Sketch hollered to his wife.

She was only a few yards away, but I wasn't going to point that out. Ash came over looking worried, but I could tell from the way she tried to school her features that she already knew.

"What?" she asked, adopting the same doe-eyed innocent look her daughters used all the time.

"Boyfriend?"

"His name is Kyle," Emmy reminded him with a toothy—though some were missing—smile.

Sketch didn't smile. Actually, he looked vaguely sick.

"Emmy, baby, why don't you go play catch with Jules?" Ash suggested.

With an exaggerated, "I guess," she waited for her dad to put her down and then took off running for her "cousins."

"Boyfriend?" Sketch repeated, patience gone.

"They're eight." Her words were reassuring, but her beleaguered expression said she knew there was no point. "He's not her boyfriend. He's a boy that played with her on the swings twice."

"Firefly, I knew you at eight. Look where we are now." He gestured at her stomach, still flat at the moment. They had announced just the week before that they were expecting again. "This little fucker is not knocking up my baby."

Once again, I felt it prudent to remove myself from a volatile conversation.

This time, I went right to my husband. He would keep me safe.

Yes, husband.

Three months ago, Stone and I had gotten married. He'd offered me a church wedding, something big and over the top, but it wasn't what I wanted. Instead, we had found a small estate about an hour away that was covered in trees and flowers. We rented it out for the day, and the whole club came to watch us exchange vows.

I'd still not found it in me to start going to church again, though my faith was stronger than ever without the corruption of the way my parents taught. After a lot of consideration, I decided I didn't want some random officiant to marry us. I'd asked Doc if he would get ordained instead, and he'd agreed right away.

It was small, intimate, casual by most standards, and it was perfect.

And when I'd walked down the makeshift aisle to Stone, I did it to "Sea of Love."

Stone was sitting, talking to Roadrunner, Cami, Tank, Quinn, and Ace. I walked up and took a seat in his lap. I'd long since learned that anything else would only result in me being moved there or right next to him, anyway.

He pressed a kiss right beneath my ear and murmured, "How's my bunny?"

"Okay," I replied. "Just trying to stop running into drama."

"Daz and Avery?" It wasn't a secret at all around the club how those two were handling the pregnancy.

"Them, and Emmy is calling some little boy her 'boyfriend,' so Sketch is freaking out."

Stone's head came up, his brow creased. "She's what?"

Seriously, all the little girls around here were going to have a very hard time of it when they started dating. All the Disciples were going to be a nightmare. Since Emmy was already flirting—and, apparently, had been since she could talk—I did not foresee good things.

"Calm down, Mr. President."

"We aren't adopting any girls," he groused.

We'd gone to see a fertility specialist a few months ago, just to discuss our options. Although there were no lasting symptoms from the gunshot wound, it was still recommended that I not try to conceive. It wouldn't be impossible, but it was highly risky. After a lot of discussion, Stone and I had decided that adopting was better for us. Since my return to work, I saw too many little ones that had no families. We could make a difference for children like that.

"Oh, we'll see," I warned. He could say whatever he wanted now, but I knew he'd melt for a little girl, just like he did for all his nieces. As a girl who'd have given anything to get that from her dad, I wanted to give someone else that chance.

He gave me a squinty-eyed look that I knew well. It was his why-do-I-always-let-you-get-your-way look. It was also all the confirmation I needed. He wouldn't dream of actually standing in the way of bringing home a little princess for us to love.

Someday, we'd make that happen. For now, there was no short supply of tiny humans to shower that affection on.

I let myself look around the yard, taking in everyone. Levi and Owen were playing catch with Gauge and Ham. Jules, now being joined by Emmy, was coloring on the patio. Evangeline was being held by a gorgeous, inked woman named Jess, who worked at Sketch's tattoo parlor as a receptionist. Ember stood next to her with Jamie in her arms. The two women next to each other looking like there might be some sort of photoshoot for a car magazine any minute. Slick was heading inside with Hunter, his son probably needing a nap. Finally, Quinn held her baby boy, Cash, just across from me while he slept.

There was a whole new generation all around us that was growing all the time. All of them would do that surrounded by something I'd dreamed of day after day.

Love. So much love it felt like a physical thing around us all.

I'd have never thought a biker clubhouse was where I would find it, but there it was.

"What's that face?"

My attention shifted to my husband looking down at me with a furrow in his brow. Always worried, ever on guard to do whatever needed to keep everyone here safe. My gruff, biker protector.

"Just happy." I gave him the truth.

He eyed me suspiciously for another moment before he let it go, pulling me in tighter to his solid chest. He could worry if he wanted, I'd long since learned there was no putting a stop to that. He would always fret, always focus on everyone else first and foremost. It was who he was. Rather than fight it, I accepted it for the show of love that it was.

Now, a year later, my body healed and my heart full, I never worried. I didn't have to. I had Stone. I had all of the Disciples. The ride might have started off scary. There may have been bumps in the road—for all of us. Whatever came next, we'd survive it, too.

In the meantime, on the back of a bike or in the clubhouse yard, I'd hold tight to my man and cruise.

COMING SOON

The end has come for the Savage Disciples MC series…

However, this won't be the end of the exploits in Hoffman.

Kate will be getting her story told to start the new
Sailor's Grave Series.

You might remember… this is the name of Sketch's tattoo
shop!

Coming Spring 2018!

ABOUT THE AUTHOR

Drew Elyse spends her days trying to convince the world that she is, in fact, a Disney Princess, and her nights writing tear-jerking and sexy romance novels.

When she isn't writing, she can usually be found over-analyzing every line of a book, binge watching a series on Netflix, doing strange vocal warm ups before singing a variety of music styles, or screaming at the TV during a Chicago Blackhawks game.

A graduate of Loyola University Chicago with a BA in English, she still lives in Chicago, IL where she was born and raised with her boyfriend and her fur babies Lola and Duncan.

Website: DrewElyse.com

Facebook: facebook.com/DrewElyseAuthor

Facebook Group: bit.ly/DisciplesClubhouse

Twitter: twitter.com/DrewElyseAuthor

Mailing List: bit.ly/DrewElyseNews

BOOKS BY DREW ELYSE

The Disciples' Daughters Series

Clutch
Shift
Engage
Ignite
Combust
Cruise

The Dissonance Series

Dissonance
Harmony

Made in the USA
Lexington, KY
13 July 2018